Prize for Music
        Leslie C. Holtham
                July 1903.

given by
    E. N. Pearson

THE HEROES

PERSEUS DELIVERING ANDROMEDA.

(From the Statue in the Louvre.)

THE HEROES

OR GREEK FAIRY TALES

FOR MY CHILDREN

BY

CHARLES KINGSLEY

LONDON
WARD, LOCK AND CO LIMITED
NEW YORK AND MELBOURNE
1900

To

MY CHILDREN

ROSE, MAURICE AND MARY

A LITTLE PRESENT OF

OLD GREEK FAIRY

TALES

Preface

MY dear Children,
Some of you have heard already of the old Greeks; and all of you, as you grow up, will hear more and more of them. Those of you who are boys will, perhaps, spend a great deal of time in reading Greek books; and the girls, though they may not learn Greek, will be sure to come across a great many stories taken from Greek history, and to see, I may say every day, things which we should not have had if it had not been for these old Greeks. You can hardly find a well-written book which has not in it Greek names, and words, and proverbs; you cannot walk through a great town without passing Greek buildings; you cannot go into a well-furnished room without seeing Greek statues and ornaments, even Greek patterns of furniture and paper; so strangely have these old Greeks left their mark behind them upon this modern

world in which we now live. And as you grow up, and read more and more, you will find that we owe to these old Greeks the beginnings of all our mathematics and geometry—that is, the science and knowledge of numbers, and of the shapes of things, and of the forces which make things move and stand at rest; and the beginnings of our geography and astronomy; and of our laws, and freedom, and politics—that is, the science of how to rule a country, and make it peaceful and strong. And we owe to them, too, the beginning of our logic—that is, the study of words and of reasoning; and of our metaphysics —that is, the study of our own thoughts and souls. And last of all, they made their language so beautiful that foreigners used to take to it instead of their own; and at last Greek became the common language of educated people all over the old world, from Persia and Egypt even to Spain and Britain. And therefore it was that the New Testament was written in Greek, that it might be read and understood by all the nations of the Roman empire; so that, next to the Jews, and the Bible which the Jews handed down to us, we owe more to these old Greeks than to any people upon earth.

Now you must remember one thing, that "Greeks" was not their real name. They called themselves always "Hellens," but the Romans miscalled them Greeks; and we have taken that wrong name from the Romans—it would take a long time to tell you why. They were made up of many tribes and many small separate states; and when you hear in this book of Minuai, and Athenians, and other such names, you must remember that they were all different tribes and peoples of the one great Hellen race, who lived in what we now call Greece, in the islands of the Archipelago, and along the coast of Asia Minor (Ionia, as they call it), from the Hellespont to Rhodes, and had afterwards colonies and cities in Sicily, and South Italy (which was called Great Greece), and along the shores of the Black Sea at Sinope, and Kertch, and at Sevastopol. And after that, again, they spread under Alexander the Great, and conquered Egypt, and Syria, and Persia, and the whole East. But that was many hundred years after my stories; for then there were no Greeks on the Black Sea shores, nor in Sicily, or Italy, or anywhere but in Greece and in Ionia. And if you are puzzled by the names of places in this book, you must take the maps and find them out. It will be a pleasanter way of learning geography than out of a dull lesson-book.

Now, I love these old Hellens heartily; and I should be very ungrateful to them if I did not, considering all that they have taught me; and they seem to me like brothers, though they have all been dead and gone many hundred years ago. So as you must learn about them, whether you choose or not, I wish to be the first to introduce you to them, and to say, "Come hither, children, at this blessed Christmas time, when all God's creatures should rejoice together, and bless Him who redeemed them all. Come and see old friends of mine, whom I knew long ere you were born. They are come to visit us at Christmas, out of the world where all live to God; and to tell you some of their old fairy tales, which they loved when they were young like you."

For nations begin at first by being children like you, though they are made up of grown men. They are children at first like you—men and women with children's hearts; frank, and affectionate, and full of trust, and teachable, and loving to see and learn all the wonders round them; and greedy also, too often, and passionate and silly, as children are.

Thus these old Greeks were teachable, and learnt from all the nations round. From the Phœnicians they learnt shipbuilding, and some say letters beside; and from the Assyrians they learnt painting, and carving, and building in wood and stone; and from the Egyptians they learnt astronomy, and many things which you would not understand. In this they were like our own forefathers the Northmen, of whom you love to hear, who, though they were wild and rough themselves, were humble, and glad to learn from every one. Therefore God rewarded these Greeks, as He rewarded our forefathers, and made them wiser than the people who taught them in everything they learnt; for He loves to see men and children open-hearted, and willing to be taught; and to him who uses what he has got, He gives more and more day by day. So these Greeks grew wise and powerful, and wrote poems which will live till the world's end, which you must read for yourselves some day, in English at least, if not in Greek. And they learnt to carve statues, and build temples, which are still among the wonders of the world; and many another wondrous thing God taught them, for which we are the wiser this day.

For you must not fancy, children, that because these old Greeks were heathens, therefore God did not care for them, and taught them nothing.

The Bible tells us that it was not so, but that God's mercy is over all His works, and that He understands the hearts of all people, and fashions all their works. And St. Paul told these old Greeks in after times, when they had grown wicked and fallen low, that they ought to have known better, because they were God's off-spring, as their own poets had said; and that the good God had put them where they were, to seek the Lord, and feel after Him, and find Him, though He was not far from any one of them. And Clement of Alexandria, a great Father of the Church, who was as wise as he was good, said that God had sent down Phil-osophy to the Greeks from heaven, as He sent down the Gospel to the Jews.

For Jesus Christ, remember, is the Light who lights every man who comes into the world. And no one can think a right thought, or feel a right feeling, or understand the real truth of anything in earth and heaven, unless the good Lord Jesus teaches him by His Spirit, which gives man understanding.

But these Greeks, as St. Paul told them, forgot what God had taught them, and, though they were God's offspring, worshipped idols of wood and stone, and fell at last into sin and shame, and then, of course, into cowardice and slavery, till they perished out of that beautiful land which God had given them for so many years.

For, like all nations who have left anything behind them, beside mere mounds of earth, they believed at first in the One True God who made all heaven and earth. But after a while, like all other nations, they began to worship other gods, or rather angels and spirits, who (so they fancied) lived about their land. Zeus, the Father of gods and men (who was some dim remembrance of the blessed true God), and Hera his wife, and Phœbus Apollo the Sun-god, and Pallas Athené who taught men wisdom and useful arts, and Aphrodite the Queen of Beauty, and Poseidon the Ruler of the Sea, and Hephaistos the King of the Fire, who taught men to work in metals. And they honoured the Gods of the Rivers, and the Nymph-maids, who they fancied lived in the caves, and the fountains, and the glens of the forest, and all beautiful wild places. And they honoured the Erinnues, the dreadful sisters, who, they thought, haunted guilty men until their sins were purged away. And many other dreams they had, which parted the One God into many; and they said, too, that these gods did things which would be a shame and sin for any man to do. And when their philosophers arose, and told them that God was One, they would not listen, but loved their idols, and their wicked idol feasts, till they all came to ruin. But we will talk of such sad things no more.

But, at the time of which this little book speaks, they had not fallen as low as that. They worshipped no idols, as far as I can find; and they still believed in the last six of the ten commandments, and knew well what was right and what was wrong. And they believed (and that was what gave them courage) that the gods loved men, and taught them, and that without the gods men were sure to come to ruin. And in that they were right enough, as we know—more right even than they thought ; for without God we can do nothing, and all wisdom comes from Him.

Now, you must not think of them in this book as learned men, living in great cities, such as they were afterwards, when they wrought all their beautiful works, but as country people, living in farms and walled villages, in a simple, hard-working way ; so that the greatest kings and heroes cooked their own meals, and thought it no shame, and made their own ships and weapons, and fed and harnessed their own horses ; and the queens worked with their maidservants, and did all the business of the house, and spun, and wove, and embroidered, and made their husbands' clothes and their own. So that a man was honoured among them, not because he happened to be rich, but according to his skill, and his strength, and courage, and the number of things which he could do. For they were but grown-up children, though they were right noble children too ; and it was with them as it is now at school—the strongest and cleverest boy, though he be poor, leads all the rest.

Now, while they were young and simple they loved fairy tales, as you do now. All nations do so when they are young : our old forefathers did, and called their stories "Sagas." I will read you some of them some day—some of the Eddas, and the Voluspà, and Beowulf, and the noble old Romances. The old Arabs, again, had their tales, which we now call the "Arabian Nights." The old Romans had theirs, and they called them "Fabulæ," from which our word "fable" comes ; but the old Hellens called theirs "Muthoi," from which our new word "myth" is taken. But next to those old Romances, which were written in the Christian middle age, there are no fairy tales like these old Greek ones, for beauty, and wisdom, and truth, and for making children love noble deeds, and trust in God to help them through.

Now, why have I called this book "The Heroes"? Because that was the name which the Hellens gave to men who were brave and skilful, and dare do more than other men. At first, I think, that was all it meant : but after a time it came to mean something more ; it came to mean men who helped their country ; men in those old times, when the country was half-wild, who killed fierce beasts and evil men, and drained swamps, and founded towns, and therefore after they were dead, were honoured, because they had left their country better than they found it. And we call such a man a hero in English to this day, and call it a " heroic " thing to suffer pain and grief, that we may do good to our fellow-men. We may all do that, my children, boys and girls alike ; and we ought to do it, for it is easier now than ever, and safer, and the path more clear. But you shall hear how the Hellens said their heroes worked, three thousand years ago. The stories are not all true, of course, nor half of them ; you are not simple enough to fancy that ; but the meaning of them is true, and true for ever, and that is—" Do right, and God will help you."

FARLEY COURT,
  Advent, 1855.

CONTENTS

STORY I.—PERSEUS

STORY II.—THE ARGONAUTS

STORY III.—THESEUS

[I OWE an apology to the few scholars who may happen to read this hasty *jeu d'esprit*, for the inconsistent method in which I have spelt Greek names. The rule which I have tried to follow has been this : when the word has been hopelessly Latinised, as "Phœbus" has been, I have left it as it usually stands ; but in other cases I have tried to keep the plain Greek spelling, except when it would have seemed pedantic, or when, as in the word "Tiphus," I should have given an altogether wrong notion of the sound of the word. It has been a choice of difficulties, which has been forced on me by our strange habit of introducing boys to the Greek myths, not in their original shape, but in a Roman disguise.]

Story I.—Perseus

PART I

ONCE upon a time there were two princes who were twins. Their names were Acrisius and Prœtus, and they lived in the pleasant vale of Argos, far away in Hellas. They had fruitful meadows and vineyards, sheep and oxen, great herds of horses feeding down in Lerna Fen, and all that men could need to make them blest : and yet they were wretched, because they were jealous of each other. From the moment they were born they began to quarrel ; and when they grew up each tried to take away the other's share of the kingdom, and keep all for himself. So first Acrisius drove out Prœtus ; and he went across the seas, and brought home a foreign princess for his wife, and foreign warriors to help him, who were called Cyclopes; and drove out Acrisius in his turn ; and then they fought a long while up and down the land, till the quarrel was settled, and Acrisius took Argos and one half the land, and Prœtus took Tiryns and the other half. And Prœtus and his Cyclopes built around Tiryns great walls of unhewn stone, which are standing to this day.

But there came a prophet to that hard-hearted Acrisius and prophesied against him, and said, " Because you have risen up against your own blood, your own blood shall rise up against you ; because you have sinned against your kindred, by your kindred you shall be punished. Your daughter Danae shall bear a son, and by that son's hands you shall die. So the Gods have ordained, and it will surely come to pass."

And at that Acrisius was very much afraid ; but he did not mend his ways. He had been cruel to his own family, and, instead of re-penting and being kind to them, he went on to be more cruel than ever : for he shut up his fair daughter Danae in a cavern underground, lined with brass, that no one might come near her. So he fancied himself more cunning than the Gods : but you will see presently whether he was able to escape them.

Now it came to pass that in time Danae bore a son ; so beautiful a babe that any but King Acrisius would have had pity on it. But he had no pity ; for he took Danae and her babe down to the seashore, and put them into a great chest and thrust them out to sea, for the winds and the waves to carry them whithersoever they would.

The north-west wind blew freshly out of the blue mountains, and down the pleasant vale of Argos, and away and out to sea. And away and out to sea before it floated the mother and her babe, while all who watched them wept, save that cruel father, King Acrisius.

So they floated on and on, and the chest danced up and down upon the billows, and the baby slept upon its mother's breast : but the poor mother could not sleep, but watched and wept, and she sang to her baby as they floated; and the song which she sang you shall learn yourselves some day.

And now they are past the last blue headland, and in the open sea ; and there is nothing round them but the waves, and the sky, and the wind. But the waves are gentle, and the sky is clear, and the breeze is tender and low; for these are the days when Halcyone and Ceyx build their nests, and no storms ever ruffle the pleasant summer sea.

And who were Halcyone and Ceyx? You shall hear while the chest floats on. Halcyone was a fairy maiden, the daughter of the beach and of the wind. And she loved a sailor-boy, and married him; and none on earth were so happy as they. But at last Ceyx was wrecked; and before he could swim to the shore the billows swallowed him up. And Halcyone saw him drowning, and leapt into the sea to him; but in vain. Then the Immortals took pity on them both, and changed them into two fair sea-birds; and now they build a floating nest every year, and sail up and down happily for ever upon the pleasant seas of Greece.

So a night passed, and a day, and a long day it was for Danae; and another night and day beside, till Danae was faint with hunger and weeping, and yet no land appeared. And all the while the babe slept quietly; and at last poor Danae dropped her head and fell asleep likewise with her cheek against the babe's.

After a while she was awakened suddenly; for the chest was jarring and grinding, and the air was full of sound. She looked up, and over her head were mighty cliffs, all red in the setting sun, and around her rocks and breakers, and flying flakes of foam. She clasped her hands together, and shrieked aloud for help. And when she cried, help met her: for now there came over the rocks a tall and stately man, and looked down wondering upon poor Danae tossing about in the chest among the waves.

He wore a rough cloak of frieze, and on his head a broad hat to shade his face; in his hand he carried a trident for spearing fish, and over his shoulder was a casting-net; but Danae could see that he was no common man by his stature, and his walk, and his flowing golden hair and beard; and by the two servants who came behind him, carrying baskets for his fish. But she had hardly time to look at him, before he had laid aside his trident and leapt down the rocks, and thrown his casting-net so surely over Danae and the chest, that he drew it, and her, and the baby, safe upon a ledge of rock.

Then the fisherman took Danae by the hand, and lifted her out of the chest, and said—

"O beautiful damsel, what strange chance has brought you to this island in so frail a ship? Who are you, and whence? Surely you are some king's daughter; and this boy has somewhat more than mortal."

And as he spoke he pointed to the babe; for its face shone like the morning star.

But Danae only held down her head, and sobbed out—

"Tell me to what land I have come, unhappy that I am; and among what men I have fallen!"

And he said, "This isle is called Seriphos, and I am a Hellen, and dwell in it. I am the brother of Polydectes the king; and men call me Dictys the netter, because I catch the fish of the shore."

Then Danae fell down at his feet, and embraced his knees, and cried—

"Oh, sir, have pity upon a stranger, whom a cruel doom has driven to your land; and let me live in your house as a servant; but treat me honourably, for I was once a king's daughter, and this my boy (as you have truly said) is of no common race. I will not be a charge to you, or eat the bread of idleness; for I am more skilful in weaving and embroidery than all the maidens of my land."

And she was going on ; but Dictys stopped her, and raised her up, and said—

" My daughter, I am old, and my hairs are growing gray; while I have no children to make my home cheerful. Come with me then, and you shall be a daughter to me and to my wife, and this babe shall be our grandchild. For I fear the Gods, and show hospitality to all strangers, knowing that good deeds, like evil ones, always return to those who do them."

So Danae was comforted, and went home with Dictys, the good fisherman, and was a daughter to him and to his wife, till fifteen years were past.

PART II

FIFTEEN years were past and gone, and
the babe was now grown to be a tall
lad and a sailor, and went many voyages after
merchandise to the islands round. His mother
called him Perseus; but all the people in Seriphos said that he was not the son of mortal
man, and called him the son of Zeus, the king
of the Immortals. For though he was but
fifteen, he was taller by a head than any man
in the island; and he was the most skilful of all
in running and wrestling and boxing, and in
throwing the quoit and the javelin, and in
rowing with the oar, and in playing on the
harp, and in all which befits a man. And
he was brave and truthful, gentle and cour-
teous, for good old Dictys had trained him
well; and well it was for Perseus that he had
done so. For now Danae and her son fell

into great danger, and Perseus had need of all his wit to defend his mother and himself.

I said that Dictys' brother was Polydectes, king of the island. He was not a righteous man, like Dictys; but greedy, and cunning, and cruel. And when he saw fair Danae, he wanted to marry her. But she would not; for she did not love him, and cared for no one but her boy, and her boy's father, whom she never hoped to see again. At last Polydectes became furious; and while Perseus was away at sea he took poor Danae away from Dictys, saying, "If you will not be my wife, you shall be my slave." So Danae was made a slave, and had to fetch water from the well, and grind in the mill, and perhaps was beaten, and wore a heavy chain, because she would not marry that cruel king. But Perseus was far away over the seas in the isle of Samos, little thinking how his mother was languishing in grief.

Now one day at Samos, while the ship was lading, Perseus wandered into a pleasant wood to get out of the sun, and sat down on the turf and fell asleep. And as he slept a strange dream came to him—the strangest dream which he had ever had in his life.

There came a lady to him through the wood, taller than he, or any mortal man ; but beautiful exceedingly, with great gray eyes, clear and piercing, but strangely soft and mild. On her head was a helmet, and in her hand a spear. And over her shoulder, above her long blue robes, hung a goat-skin, which bore up a mighty shield of brass, polished like a mirror. She stood and looked at him with her clear gray eyes; and Perseus saw that her eyelids never moved, nor her eyeballs, but looked straight through and through him, and into his very heart, as if she could see all the secrets of his soul, and knew all that he had ever thought or longed for since the day that he was born. And Perseus dropped his eyes, trembling and blushing, as the wonderful lady spoke.

"Perseus, you must do an errand for me."

"Who are you, lady ? And how do you know my name ?"

"I am Pallas Athené ; and I know the thoughts of all men's hearts, and discern their manhood or their baseness. And from the souls of clay I turn away, and they are blest, but not by me. They fatten at ease, like sheep in the pasture, and eat what they did not sow,

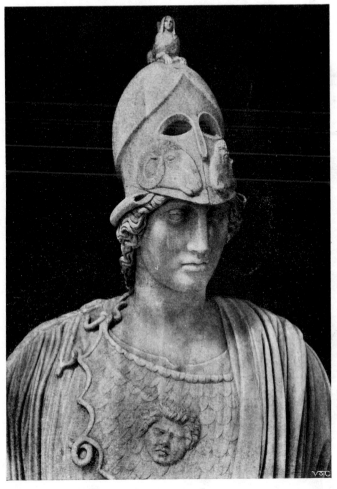

PALLAS ATHENÉ.

(From a Statue in the Vatican.)

like oxen in the stall. They grow and spread, like the gourd along the ground ; but, like the gourd, they give no shade to the traveller, and when they are ripe death gathers them, and they go down unloved into hell, and their name vanishes out of the land.

"But to the souls of fire I give more fire, and to those who are manful I give a might more than man's. These are the heroes, the sons of the Immortals, who are blest, but not like the souls of clay. For I drive them forth by strange paths, Perseus, that they may fight the Titans and the monsters, the enemies of Gods and men. Through doubt and need, danger and battle, I drive them ; and some of them are slain in the flower of youth, no man knows when or where ; and some of them win noble names, and a fair and green old age ; but what will be their latter end I know not, and none, save Zeus, the father of Gods and men. Tell me now, Perseus, which of these two sorts of men seem to you more blest ? "

Then Perseus answered boldly : " Better to die in the flower of youth, on the chance of winning a noble name, than to live at ease like the sheep, and die unloved and unrenowned."

C

Then that strange lady laughed, and held up her brazen shield, and cried : "See here, Perseus; dare you face such a monster as this, and slay it, that I may place its head upon this shield ? "

And in the mirror of the shield there appeared a face, and as Perseus looked on it his blood ran cold. It was the face of a beautiful woman ; but her cheeks were pale as death, and her brows were knit with everlasting pain, and her lips were thin and bitter like a snake's ; and instead of hair, vipers wreathed about her temples, and shot out their forked tongues ; while round her head were folded wings like an eagle's, and upon her bosom claws of brass.

And Perseus looked awhile, and then said : "If there is anything so fierce and foul on earth, it were a noble deed to kill it. Where can I find the monster ? "

Then the strange lady smiled again, and said : "Not yet; you are too young, and too unskilled ; for this is Medusa the Gorgon, the mother of a monstrous brood. Return to your home, and do the work which waits there for you. You must play the man in that before I can think you worthy to go in search of the Gorgon."

Then Perseus would have spoken, but the strange lady vanished, and he awoke; and behold, it was a dream. But day and night Perseus saw before him the face of that dreadful woman, with the vipers writhing round her head.

So he returned home; and when he came to Seriphos, the first thing which he heard was that his mother was a slave in the house of Polydectes.

Grinding his teeth with rage, he went out, and away to the king's palace, and through the men's rooms, and the women's rooms, and so through all the house (for no one dared stop him, so terrible and fair was he), till he found his mother sitting on the floor, turning the stone hand-mill, and weeping as she turned it. And he lifted her up, and kissed her, and bade her follow him forth. But before they could pass out of the room Polydectes came in, raging. And when Perseus saw him, he flew upon him as the mastiff flies on the boar. "Villain and tyrant!" he cried; "is this your respect for the Gods, and thy mercy to strangers and widows? You shall die!" And because he had no sword he caught up the stone hand-mill, and lifted it to dash out Poly-dectes' brains.

But his mother clung to him, shrieking, "Oh, my son, we are strangers and helpless in the land; and if you kill the king, all the people will fall on us, and we shall both die."

Good Dictys, too, who had come in, entreated him. "Remember that he is my brother. Remember how I have brought you up, and trained you as my own son, and spare him for my sake."

Then Perseus lowered his hand; and Poly-dectes, who had been trembling all this while like a coward, because he knew that he was in the wrong, let Perseus and his mother pass.

Perseus took his mother to the temple of Athené, and there the priestess made her one of the temple-sweepers; for there they knew she would be safe, and not even Polydectes would dare to drag her away from the altar. And there Perseus, and the good Dictys, and his wife, came to visit her every day; while Polydectes, not being able to get what he wanted by force, cast about in his wicked heart how he might get it by cunning.

Now he was sure that he could never get

back Danae as long as Perseus was in the
island; so he made a plot to rid himself of
him. And first he pretended to have forgiven
Perseus, and to have forgotten Danae; so that,
for a while, all went as smoothly as ever.

Next he proclaimed a great feast, and invited
to it all the chiefs, and landowners, and the
young men of the island, and among them
Perseus, that they might all do him homage as
their king, and eat of his banquet in his hall.

On the appointed day they all came; and as
the custom was then, each guest brought his
present with him to the king : one a horse,
another a shawl, or a ring, or a sword; and
those who had nothing better brought a basket
of grapes, or of game; but Perseus brought
nothing, for he had nothing to bring, being but
a poor sailor-lad.

He was ashamed, however, to go into the
king's presence without his gift; and he was
too proud to ask Dictys to lend him one. So
he stood at the door sorrowfully, watching the
rich men go in ; and his face grew very red as
they pointed at him, and smiled, and whispered,
" What has that foundling to give ? "

Now this was what Polydectes wanted ; and

as soon as he heard that Perseus stood without, he bade them bring him in, and asked him scornfully before them all, "Am I not your king, Perseus, and have I not invited you to my feast? Where is your present, then?"

Perseus blushed and stammered, while all the proud men round laughed, and some of them began jeering him openly. "This fellow was thrown ashore here like a piece of weed or drift-wood, and yet he is too proud to bring a gift to the king."

"And though he does not know who his father is, he is vain enough to let the old women call him the son of Zeus."

And so forth, till poor Perseus grew mad with shame, and hardly knowing what he said, cried out,—"A present! who are you who talk of presents? See if I do not bring a nobler one than all of yours together!"

So he said boasting; and yet he felt in his heart that he was braver than all those scoffers, and more able to do some glorious deed.

"Hear him! Hear the boaster! What is it to be?" cried they all, laughing louder than ever.

Then his dream at Samos came into his

mind, and he cried aloud, " The head of the Gorgon."

He was half afraid after he had said the words ; for all laughed louder than ever, and Polydectes loudest of all.

" You have promised to bring me the Gorgon's head ? Then never appear again in this island without it. Go ! "

Perseus ground his teeth with rage, for he saw that he had fallen into a trap ; but his promise lay upon him, and he went out without a word.

Down to the cliffs he went, and looked across the broad blue sea ; and he wondered if his dream were true, and prayed in the bitterness of his soul.

" Pallas Athené, was my dream true ? and shall I slay the Gorgon ? If thou didst really show me her face, let me not come to shame as a liar and boastful. Rashly and angrily I promised ; but cunningly and patiently will I perform."

But there was no answer, nor sign ; neither thunder nor any appearance ; not even a cloud in the sky.

And three times Perseus called weeping,

" Rashly and angrily I promised ; but cunningly and patiently will I perform."

Then he saw afar off above the seas a small white cloud, as bright as silver. And it came on, nearer and nearer, till its brightness dazzled his eyes.

Perseus wondered at that strange cloud, for there was no other cloud all round the sky ; and he trembled as it touched the cliff below. And as it touched, it broke, and parted, and within it appeared Pallas Athené, as he had seen her at Samos in his dream, and beside her a young man more light-limbed than the stag, whose eyes were like sparks of fire. By his side was a scimitar of diamond, all of one clear precious stone, and on his feet were golden sandals, from the heels of which grew living wings.

They looked upon Perseus keenly, and yet they never moved their eyes ; and they came up the cliffs towards him more swiftly than the sea-gull, and yet they never moved their feet, nor did the breeze stir the robes about their limbs ; only the wings of the youth's sandals quivered, like a hawk's when he hangs above the cliff. And Perseus fell down and worshipped, for he knew that they were more than men.

But Athené stood before him and spoke gently, and bid him have no fear. Then—

" Perseus," she said, " he who overcomes in one trial merits thereby a sharper trial still. You have braved Polydectes, and done manfully. Dare you brave Medusa the Gorgon ? "

And Perseus said, " Try me ; for since you spoke to me in Samos a new soul has come into my breast, and I should be ashamed not to dare anything which I can do. Show me, then, how I can do this ! "

" Perseus," said Athené, " think well before you attempt ; for this deed requires a seven years' journey, in which you cannot repent or turn back nor escape ; but if your heart fails you, you must die in the Unshapen Land, where no man will ever find your bones."

" Better so than live here, useless and despised," said Perseus. " Tell me, then, oh tell me, fair and wise Goddess, of your great kindness and condescension, how I can do but this one thing, and then, if need be, die ! "

Then Athené smiled and said—

" Be patient, and listen ; for if you forget

my words, you will indeed die. You must go northward to the country of the Hyperboreans, who live beyond the pole, at the sources of the cold north wind, till you find the three Gray Sisters, who have but one eye and one tooth between them. You must ask them the way to the Nymphs, the daughters of the Evening Star, who dance about the golden tree, in the Atlantic island of the west. They will tell you the way to the Gorgon, that you may slay her, my enemy, the mother of monstrous beasts. Once she was a maiden as beautiful as morn, till in her pride she sinned a sin at which the sun hid his face ; and from that day her hair was turned to vipers, and her hands to eagle's claws ; and her heart was filled with shame and rage, and her lips with bitter venom ; and her eyes became so terrible that whosoever looks on them is turned to stone ; and her children are the winged horse and the giant of the golden sword ; and her grandchildren are Echidna the witch-adder, and Geryon the three-headed tyrant, who feeds his herds beside the herds of hell. So she became the sister of the Gorgons, Stheino and Euryte the abhorred,

the daughters of the Queen of the Sea.
Touch them not, for they are immortal; but
bring me only Medusa's head."

"And I will bring it!" said Perseus; "but
how am I to escape her eyes? Will she not
freeze me too into stone?"

"You shall take this polished shield," said
Athené, "and when you come near her look
not at her herself, but at her image in the
brass; so you may strike her safely. And
when you have struck off her head, wrap it,
with your face turned away, in the folds of the
goat-skin on which the shield hangs, the hide
of Amaltheié, the nurse of the Ægis-holder.
So you will bring it safely back to me, and win
to yourself renown, and a place among the
heroes who feast with the Immortals upon the
peak where no winds blow."

Then Perseus said, "I will go, though I die
in going. But how shall I cross the seas
without a ship? And who will show me my
way? And when I find her, how shall I slay
her, if her scales be iron and brass?"

Then the young man spoke: "These sandals
of mine will bear you across the seas, and over
hill and dale like a bird, as they bear me all

day long; for I am Hermes, the far-famed Argus-slayer, the messenger of the Immortals who dwell on Olympus."

Then Perseus fell down and worshipped, while the young man spoke again :

"The sandals themselves will guide you on the road, for they are divine and cannot stray ; and this sword itself, the Argus-slayer, will kill her, for it is divine, and needs no second stroke. Arise, and gird them on, and go forth."

So Perseus arose, and girded on the sandals and the sword.

And Athené cried, " Now leap from the cliff and be gone."

But Perseus lingered.

"May I not bid farewell to my mother and to Dictys ? And may I not offer burnt-offerings to you, and to Hermes the far-famed Argus-slayer, and to Father Zeus above ? "

"You shall not bid farewell to your mother, lest your heart relent at her weeping. I will comfort her and Dictys until you return in peace. Nor shall you offer burnt-offerings to the Olympians ; for your offering shall be Medusa's head. Leap, and trust in the armour of the Immortals."

Then Perseus looked down the cliff and shuddered ; but he was ashamed to show his dread. Then he thought of Medusa and the renown before him, and he leaped into the empty air.

And behold, instead of falling he floated, and stood, and ran along the sky. He looked back, but Athené had vanished, and Hermes ; and the sandals led him on northward ever, like a crane who follows the spring toward the Ister fens.

PART III

SO Perseus started on his journey, going dry-shod over land and sea; and his heart was high and joyful, for the winged sandals bore him each day a seven days' journey.

And he went by Cythnus, and by Ceos, and the pleasant Cyclades to Attica; and past Athens and Thebes, and the Copaic lake, and up the vale of Cephissus, and past the peaks of Œta and Pindus, and over the rich Thessalian plains, till the sunny hills of Greece were behind him, and before him were the wilds of the north. Then he passed the Thracian mountains, and many a barbarous tribe, Pæons and Dardans and Triballi, till he came to the Ister stream, and the dreary Scythian plains. And he walked across the Ister dry-shod, and away through the moors and fens, day and night toward the bleak north-west, turning neither to the right hand nor the left, till he came to the Unshapen Land, and the place which has no name.

And seven days he walked through it, on a path which few can tell; for those who have trodden it like least to speak of it, and those who go there again in dreams are glad enough when they awake; till he came to the edge of the everlasting night, where the air was full of feathers, and the soil was hard with ice; and there at last he found the three Gray Sisters, by the shore of the freezing sea, nodding upon a white log of drift-wood, beneath the cold white winter moon; and they chaunted a low song together, "Why the old times were better than the new."

There was no living thing around them, not a fly, not a moss upon the rocks. Neither seal nor sea-gull dare come near, lest the ice should clutch them in its claws. The surge broke up in foam, but it fell again in flakes of snow; and it frosted the hair of the three Gray Sisters, and the bones in the ice-cliff above their heads. They passed the eye from one to the other, but for all that they could not see; and they passed the tooth from one to the other, but for all that they could not eat; and they sat in the full glare of the moon, but they were none the warmer for her beams. And Perseus pitied the three Gray Sisters; but they did not pity themselves.

So he said, " Oh, venerable mothers, wisdom is the daughter of old age. You therefore should know many things. Tell me, if you can, the path to the Gorgon."

Then one cried, " Who is this who reproaches us with old age?" And another, " This is the voice of one of the children of men."

And he, " I do not reproach, but honour your old age, and I am one of the sons of men and of the heroes. The rulers of Olympus have sent me to you to ask the way to the Gorgon."

Then one, " There are new rulers in Olympus, and all new things are bad." And another, " We hate your rulers, and the heroes, and all the children of men. We are the kindred of the Titans, and the Giants, and the Gorgons, and the ancient monsters of the deep." And another, " Who is this rash and insolent man who pushes unbidden into our world?" And the first, " There never was such a world as ours, nor will be ; if we let him see it, he will spoil it all."

Then one cried, " Give me the eye, that I may see him ; " and another, " Give me the tooth, that I may bite him." But Perseus, when he saw that they were foolish and proud, and did not love the children of men, left off pitying them, and said to himself, " Hungry men must needs be hasty; if I stay making words here, I shall be starved." Then he stepped close to them, and watched till they passed the eye from hand to hand. And as they groped about between themselves, he held out his hand gently, till one of them put the eye into it, fancying that it was the hand of her sister. Then he sprang back, and laughed, and cried—

" Cruel and proud old women, I have your eye ; and I will throw it into the sea, unless you tell me the path to the Gorgon, and swear to me that you tell me right."

Then they wept, and chattered, and scolded ; but in vain. They were forced to tell the truth, though, when they told it, Perseus could hardly make out the road.

D

"You must go," they said, "foolish boy, to the southward, into the ugly glare of the sun, till you come to Atlas the Giant, who holds the heaven and the earth apart. And you must ask his daughters, the Hesperides, who are young and foolish like yourself. And now give us back our eye, for we have forgotten all the rest."

So Perseus gave them back their eye; but instead of using it, they nodded and fell fast asleep, and were turned into blocks of ice, till the tide came up and washed them all away. And now they float up and down like icebergs for ever, weeping whenever they meet the sunshine, and the fruitful summer, and the warm south wind, which fill young hearts with joy.

But Perseus leaped away to the southward, leaving the snow and the ice behind: past the isle of the Hyperboreans, and the tin isles, and the long Iberian shore, while the sun rose higher day by day upon a bright blue summer sea. And the terns and the sea-gulls swept laughing round his head, and called to him to stop and play, and the dolphins gambolled up as he passed, and offered to carry him on their backs. And all night long the sea-nymphs sang sweetly, and the Tritons blew upon their conchs, as they played round Galatæa their queen, in her car of pearled shells. Day by day the sun rose higher, and leaped more swiftly into the sea at night, and more swiftly out of the sea at dawn; while Perseus skimmed over the billows like a sea-gull, and his feet were never wetted; and leapt on from wave to wave, and his limbs were never weary, till he saw far away a mighty mountain, all rose-red in the setting sun. Its feet were wrapped in forests, and its head in wreaths of cloud; and Perseus knew that it was Atlas, who holds the heavens and the earth apart.

He came to the mountain, and leapt on shore, and wandered upward, among pleasant valleys and waterfalls, and tall trees and strange ferns and flowers; but there was no smoke rising from any glen, nor house, nor sign of man.

At last he heard sweet voices singing; and he guessed that he was come to the garden of the Nymphs, the daughters of the Evening Star.

They sang like nightingales among the thickets, and Perseus stopped to hear their song; but the words which they spoke he could not understand; no, nor no man after him for many a hundred years. So he stepped forward and saw them dancing, hand in hand around the charmed tree, which bent under its golden fruit; and round the tree-foot was coiled the dragon, old Ladon the sleepless snake, who lies there for ever, listening to the song of the maidens, blinking and watching with dry bright eyes.

Then Perseus stopped, not because he feared the dragon, but because he was bashful before those fair maids; but when they saw him, they too stopped, and called to him with trembling voices—

"Who are you? Are you Heracles the mighty, who will come to rob our garden, and carry off our golden fruit?" And he answered—

"I am not Heracles the mighty, and I want none of your golden fruit. Tell me, fair Nymphs, the way which leads to the Gorgon, that I may go on my way and slay her."

"Not yet, not yet, fair boy; come dance with us around the tree in the garden which knows no winter, the home of the south wind and the sun. Come hither and play with us awhile; we have danced alone here for a thousand years, and our hearts are weary with longing for a playfellow. So come, come, come!"

"I cannot dance with you, fair maidens; for I must do the errand of the Immortals. So tell me the way to the Gorgon, lest I wander and perish in the waves."

Then they sighed and wept; and answered—

"The Gorgon! she will freeze you into stone."

"It is better to die like a hero than to live like an ox in a stall. The Immortals have lent me weapons, and they will give me wit to use them."

Then they sighed again and answered, "Fair boy, if you are bent on your own ruin, be it so. We know not the way to the Gorgon; but we will ask the giant Atlas, above upon the mountain peak, the brother of our father, the silver Evening Star. He sits aloft and sees across the ocean, and far away into the Unshapen Land."

So they went up the mountain to Atlas their uncle, and Perseus went up with them. And they found the giant kneeling, as he held the heavens and the earth apart.

They asked him, and he answered mildly, pointing to the sea-board with his mighty hand, "I can see the Gorgons lying on an island far away, but this youth can never come near them, unless he has the hat of darkness, which whosoever wears cannot be seen."

Then cried Perseus, "Where is that hat, that I may find it?"

But the giant smiled. "No living mortal can find that hat, for it lies in the depths of Hades, in the regions of the dead. But my nieces are immortal, and they shall fetch it for you, if you will promise me one thing and keep your faith."

Then Perseus promised; and the giant said, "When you come back with the head of Medusa, you shall show me the beautiful horror, that I may lose my feeling and my breathing, and become a stone for ever; for it is weary labour for me to hold the heavens and the earth apart."

Then Perseus promised, and the eldest of the Nymphs went down, and into a dark cavern among the cliffs, out of which came smoke and thunder, for it was one of the mouths of Hell.

And Perseus and the Nymphs sat down seven days, and waited trembling, till the Nymph came up again; and her face was pale, and her eyes dazzled with the light, for she had been long in the dreary darkness; but in her hand was the magic hat.

Then all the Nymphs kissed Perseus, and wept over him a long while; but he was only impatient to be gone. And at last they put the hat upon his head, and he vanished out of their sight.

But Perseus went on boldly, past many an ugly sight, far away into the heart of the Un-shapen Land, beyond the streams of Ocean, to the isles where no ship cruises, where is neither night nor day, where nothing is in its right place, and nothing has a name; till he heard the rustle of the Gorgons' wings and saw the glitter of their brazen talons; and then he knew that it was time to halt, lest Medusa should freeze him into stone.

He thought awhile with himself, and remembered Athené's words. He rose aloft into the air, and held the mirror of the shield above his head, and looked up into it that he might see all that was below him.

And he saw the three Gorgons sleeping, as huge as elephants. He knew that they could not see him, because the hat of darkness hid him; and yet he trembled as he sank down near them, so terrible were those brazen claws.

Two of the Gorgons were foul as swine, and lay sleeping heavily, as swine sleep, with their mighty wings outspread; but Medusa tossed to and fro restlessly, and as she tossed Perseus pitied her, she looked so fair and sad. Her plumage was like the rainbow, and her face was like the face of a nymph, only her eyebrows were knit, and her lips clenched, with everlasting care and pain; and her long neck gleamed so white in the mirror that Perseus had not the heart to strike, and said, " Ah, that it had been either of her sisters ! "

But as he looked, from among her tresses

PERSEUS WITH THE HEAD OF MEDUSA.
(From the Statue by Cellini, at Florence)

the vipers' heads awoke, and peeped up with their bright dry eyes, and showed their fangs, and hissed; and Medusa, as she tossed, threw back her wings and showed her brazen claws; and Perseus saw that, for all her beauty, she was as foul and venomous as the rest.

Then he came down and stepped to her boldly, and looked steadfastly on his mirror, and struck with Herpé stoutly once; and he did not need to strike again.

Then he wrapped the head in the goat-skin, turning away his eyes, and sprang into the air aloft faster than he ever sprang before.

For Medusa's wings and talons rattled as she sank dead upon the rocks; and her two foul sisters woke, and saw her lying dead.

Into the air they sprang yelling, and looked for him who had done the deed. Thrice they swung round and round, like hawks who beat for a partridge; and thrice they snuffed round and round, like hounds who draw upon a deer. At last they struck upon the scent of the blood, and they checked for a moment to make sure; and then on they rushed with a fearful howl, while the wind rattled hoarse in their wings.

On they rushed, sweeping and flapping, like eagles after a hare; and Perseus' blood ran cold, for all his courage, as he saw them come howling on his track; and he cried, "Bear me up well now, brave sandals, for the hounds of Death are at my heels!"

And well the brave sandals bore him, aloft through cloud and sunshine, across the shoreless sea; and fast followed the hounds of Death, as the roar of their wings came down the wind. But the roar came down fainter and fainter, and the howl of their voices died away; for the sandals were too swift, even for Gorgons, and by nightfall they were far behind, two black specks in the southern sky, till the sun sank and he saw them no more.

Then he came again to Atlas, and the garden of the Nymphs; and when the giant heard him coming, he groaned, and said, "Fulfil thy promise to me." Then Perseus held up to him the Gorgon's head, and he had rest from all his toil; for he became a crag of stone, which sleeps for ever far above the clouds.

Then he thanked the Nymphs, and asked them, "By what road shall I go homeward again, for I wandered far round in coming hither?"

And they wept and cried, "Go home no more, but stay and play with us, the lonely maidens, who dwell for ever far away from Gods and men."

But he refused, and they told him his road, and said, "Take with you this magic fruit, which, if you eat once, you will not hunger for seven days. For you must go eastward and eastward ever, over the doleful Lybian shore, which Poseidon gave to Father Zeus, when he burst open the Bosphorus and the Hellespont, and drowned the fair Lectonian land. And Zeus took that land in exchange, a fair bargain, much bad ground for a little good, and to this day it lies waste and desert, with shingle, and rock, and sand."

Then they kissed Perseus, and wept over him, and he leapt down the mountain, and went on, lessening and lessening like a sea-gull, away and out to sea.

PART IV

SO Perseus flitted onward to the north-east, over many a league of sea, till he came to the rolling sand-hills and the dreary Lybian shore.

And he flitted on across the desert: over rock-ledges, and banks of shingle, and level wastes of sand, and shell-drifts bleaching in the sunshine, and the skeletons of great sea-monsters, and dead bones of ancient giants, strewn up and down upon the old sea-floor. And as he went the blood-drops fell to the earth from the Gorgon's head, and became poisonous asps and adders, which breed in the desert to this day.

Over the sands he went,—he never knew how far or how long, feeding on the fruit which the Nymphs had given him, till he saw the hills of the Psylli, and the Dwarfs who fought with cranes. Their spears were of reeds and rushes, and their houses of the egg-shells of the cranes ; and Perseus laughed, and went his way to the north-east, hoping all day long to see the blue Mediterranean sparkling, that he might fly across it to his home.

But now came down a mighty wind, and swept him back southward toward the desert. All day long he strove against it ; but even the winged sandals could not prevail. So he was forced to float down the wind all night ; and when the morning dawned there was nothing to be seen, save the same old hateful waste of sand.

And out of the north the sandstorms rushed upon him, blood-red pillars and wreaths, blotting out the noonday sun ; and Perseus fled before them, lest he should be choked by the burning dust. At last the gale fell calm, and he tried to go northward again ; but again came down the sandstorms, and swept him back into the waste, and then all was calm and cloudless as before. Seven days he strove against the storms, and seven days he was driven back, till he was spent with thirst and hunger, and his tongue clove to the roof of his mouth. Here and there he fancied that he saw a fair lake, and the sunbeams shining on the water ; but when he came to it it vanished at his feet, and there was nought but burning sand. And if he had not been of the race of the Immortals, he would have perished in the waste ; but his life was strong within him, because it was more than man's.

Then he cried to Athené, and said—

" Oh, fair and pure, if thou hearest me, wilt thou leave me here to die of drought ? I have brought thee the Gorgon's head at thy bidding, and hitherto thou hast prospered my journey ; dost thou desert me at the last ? Else why will not these immortal sandals prevail, even against the desert storms ? Shall I never see my mother more, and the blue ripple round Seriphos, and the sunny hills of Hellas ? "

So he prayed ; and after he had prayed there was a great silence.

The heaven was still above his head, and the sand was still beneath his feet; and Perseus looked up, but there was nothing but the blinding sun in the blinding blue ; and round him, but there was nothing but the blinding sand.

And Perseus stood still a while, and waited, and said, " Surely I am not here without the will of the Immortals, for Athené will not lie. Were not these sandals to lead me in the right road ? Then the road in which I have tried to go must be a wrong road."

Then suddenly his ears were opened, and he heard the sound of running water.

And at that his heart was lifted up, though he scarcely dare believe his ears ; and weary as he was, he hurried forward, though he could scarcely stand upright ; and within a bowshot of him was a glen in the sand, and marble rocks, and date-trees, and a lawn of gay green grass. And through the lawn a streamlet sparkled and wandered out beyond the trees, and vanished in the sand.

The water trickled among the rocks, and a pleasant breeze rustled in the dry date-branches ; and Perseus laughed for joy, and leapt down the cliff, and drank of the cool water, and ate of the dates, and slept upon the turf, and leapt up and went forward again : but not toward the north this time; for he said, "Surely Athené hath sent me hither, and will not have me go homeward yet. What if there be another noble deed to be done, before I see the sunny hills of Hellas ? "

So he went east, and east for ever, by fresh oases and fountains, date-palms, and lawns of grass, till he saw before him a mighty mountain-wall, all rose-red in the setting sun.

Then he towered in the air like an eagle, for his limbs were strong again ; and he flew all night across the mountain till the day began to dawn, and rosy-fingered Eos came blushing up the sky. And then, behold, beneath him was the long green garden of Egypt and the shining stream of Nile.

And he saw cities walled up to heaven, and temples, and obelisks, and pyramids, and giant Gods of stone. And he came down amid fields of barley, and flax, and millet, and clambering gourds ; and saw the people coming out of the gates of a great city, and setting to work, each in his place, among the water-courses, parting the streams among the plants cunningly with their feet, according to the wisdom of the Egyptians. But when they saw him they all stopped their work, and gathered round him and cried—

"Who art thou, fair youth ? and what bearest thou beneath thy goat-skin there ? Surely thou art one of the Immortals ; for thy skin is white like ivory, and ours is red like clay. Thy hair is like threads of gold, and ours is black and curled. Surely thou art one of the Immortals ; " and they would have worshipped him then and there ; but Perseus said—

" I am not one of the Immortals ; but I am a hero of the Hellens. And I have slain the Gorgon in the wilderness, and bear her head with me. Give me food, therefore, that I may go forward and finish my work."

Then they gave him food, and fruit, and wine ; but they would not let him go. And when the news came into the city that the Gorgon was slain, the priests came out to meet him, and the maidens, with songs and dances, and timbrels and harps ; and they would have brought him to their temple and to their king ; but Perseus put on the hat of darkness, and vanished away out of their sight.

Therefore the Egyptians looked long for his return, but in vain, and worshipped him as a hero, and made a statue of him in Chemmis, which stood for many a hundred years ; and they said that he appeared to them at times, with sandals a cubit long ; and that whenever

E

he appeared the season was fruitful, and the Nile rose high that year.

Then Perseus went to the eastward, along the Red Sea shore ; and then, because he was afraid to go into the Arabian deserts, he turned northward once more, and this time no storm hindered him.

He went past the Isthmus, and Mount Casius, and the vast Serbonian bog, and up the shore of Palestine, where the dark-faced Æthiops dwelt.

He flew on past pleasant hills and valleys, like Argos itself, or Lacedæmon, or the fair Vale of Tempe. But the lowlands were all drowned by floods, and the highlands blasted by fire, and the hills heaved like a bubbling cauldron, before the wrath of King Poseidon, the shaker of the earth.

And Perseus feared to go inland, but flew along the shore above the sea ; and he went on all the day, and the sky was black with smoke ; and he went on all the night, and the sky was red with flame.

And at the dawn of day he looked toward the cliffs ; and at the water's edge, under a black rock, he saw a white image stand.

" This," thought he, " must surely be the statue of some sea-God ; I will go near and see what kind of Gods these barbarians worship."

So he came near ; but when he came, it was no statue, but a maiden of flesh and blood ; for he could see her tresses streaming in the breeze; and as he came closer still, he could see how she shrank and shivered when the waves sprinkled her with cold salt spray. Her arms were spread above her head, and fastened to the rock with chains of brass ; and her head drooped on her bosom, either with sleep, or weariness, or grief. But now and then she looked up and wailed, and called her mother ; yet she did not see Perseus, for the cap of darkness was on his head.

Full of pity and indignation, Perseus drew near and looked upon the maid. Her cheeks were darker than his were, and her hair was blue-black like a hyacinth; but Perseus thought, " I have never seen so beautiful a maiden ; no, not in all our isles. Surely she is a king's daughter. Do barbarians treat their kings' daughters thus ? She is too fair, at least, to have done any wrong. I will speak to her."

And, lifting the hat from his head, he flashed into her sight. She shrieked with terror, and tried to hide her face with her hair, for she could not with her hands ; but Perseus cried—

"Do not fear me, fair one ; I am a Hellen, and no barbarian. What cruel men have bound you ? But first I will set you free."

And he tore at the fetters, but they were too strong for him ; while the maiden cried—

"Touch me not ; I am accursed, devoted as a victim to the sea-Gods. They will slay you, if you dare to set me free."

"Let them try," said Perseus ; and drawing Herpé from his thigh, he cut through the brass as if it had been flax.

"Now," he said, "you belong to me, and not to these sea-Gods, whosoever they may be !" But she only called the more on her mother.

"Why call on your mother ? She can be no mother to have left you here. If a bird is dropped out of the nest, it belongs to the man who picks it up. If a jewel is cast by the way-side, it is his who dare win it and wear it, as I will win you and will wear you. I know now why Pallas Athené sent me hither. She sent me to gain a prize worth all my toil and more."

And he clasped her in his arms and cried, "Where are these sea-Gods, cruel and unjust, who doom fair maids to death? I carry the weapons of the Immortals. Let them measure their strength against mine! But tell me, maiden, who you are, and what dark fate brought you here."

And she answered, weeping—

"I am the daughter of Cepheus, King of Iopa, and my mother is Cassiopœia of the beautiful tresses, and they called me Andromeda, as long as life was mine. And I stand bound here, hapless that I am, for the sea-monster's food, to atone for my mother's sin. For she boasted of me once that I was fairer than Atergatis, Queen of the Fishes; so she in her wrath sent the sea-floods, and her brother the Fire King sent the earthquakes, and wasted all the land, and after the floods a monster bred of the slime, who devours all living things. And now he must devour me, guiltless though I am—me who never harmed a living thing, nor saw a fish upon the shore but I gave it life, and threw it back into the sea; for in our land we

eat no fish, for fear of Atergatis their queen.
Yet the priests say that nothing but my blood
can atone for a sin which I never committed."

But Perseus laughed, and said, "A sea-
monster? I have fought with worse than him :
I would have faced Immortals for your sake ;
how much more a beast of the sea ? "

Then Andromeda looked up at him, and new
hope was kindled in her breast, so proud and
fair did he stand, with one hand round her, and
in the other the glittering sword. But she only
sighed, and wept the more, and cried—

"Why will you die, young as you are ? Is
there not death and sorrow enough in the world
already? It is noble for me to die, that I may
save the lives of a whole people ; but you, better
than them all, why should I slay you too ? Go
you your way, I must go mine."

But Perseus cried, " Not so; for the Lords of
Olympus, whom I serve, are the friends of the
heroes, and help them on to noble deeds. Led
by them, I slew the Gorgon, the beautiful
horror ; and not without them do I come hither,
to slay this monster with the same Gorgon's
head. Yet hide your eyes when I leave you,
lest the sight of it freeze you too to stone."

But the maiden answered nothing, for she could not believe his words. And then, suddenly looking up, she pointed to the sea, and shrieked—

"There he comes, with the sunrise, as they promised. I must die now. How shall I endure it? Oh, go! Is it not dreadful enough to be torn piecemeal, without having you to look on?" And she tried to thrust him away.

But he said, "I go; yet promise me one thing ere I go: that if I slay this beast you will be my wife, and come back with me to my kingdom in fruitful Argos, for I am a king's heir. Promise me, and seal it with a kiss."

Then she lifted up her face, and kissed him; and Perseus laughed for joy, and flew upward, while Andromeda crouched trembling on the rock, waiting for what might befall.

On came the great sea-monster, coasting along like a huge black galley, lazily breasting the ripple, and stopping at times by creek or headland to watch for the laughter of girls at their bleaching, or cattle pawing on the sandhills, or boys bathing on the beach. His great sides were fringed with clustering shells and sea-weeds, and the water gurgled in and out of his wide jaws, as he rolled along, dripping and glistening in the beams of the morning sun.

At last he saw Andromeda, and shot forward to take his prey, while the waves foamed white behind him, and before him the fish fled leaping.

Then down from the height of the air fell Perseus like a shooting star; down to the crests of the waves, while Andromeda hid her face as he shouted; and then there was silence for a while.

At last she looked up trembling, and saw Perseus springing toward her; and instead of the monster a long black rock, with the sea rippling quietly round it.

Who then so proud as Perseus, as he leapt back to the rock, and lifted his fair Andromeda in his arms, and flew with her to the cliff-top, as a falcon carries a dove?

Who so proud as Perseus, and who so joyful as all the Æthiop people? For they had stood watching the monster from the cliffs, wailing for the maiden's fate. And already a messenger had gone to Cepheus and Cassiopœia, where they sat in sackcloth and ashes on the ground, in the innermost palace chambers, awaiting their daughter's end. And they came, and all the city with them, to see the wonder, with songs and with dances, with cymbals and harps, and received their daughter back again, as one alive from the dead.

Then Cepheus said, " Hero of the Hellens, stay here with me and be my son-in-law, and I will give you the half of my kingdom."

" I will be your son-in-law," said Perseus, "but of your kingdom I will have none, for I long after the pleasant land of Greece, and my mother who waits for me at home."

Then Cepheus said, " You must not take my daughter away at once, for she is to us like one alive from the dead. Stay with us here a year, and after that you shall return with honour." And Perseus consented ; but before he went to the palace he bade the people bring stones and wood, and built three altars, one to Athené, and one to Hermes, and one to Father Zeus, and offered bullocks and rams.

And some said, " This is a pious man ; " yet the priests said, " The Sea Queen will be yet more fierce against us, because her monster is slain." But they were afraid to speak aloud, for they feared the Gorgon's head. So they went up to the palace ; and when they came in, there stood in the hall Phineus, the brother of Cepheus, chafing like a bear robbed of her whelps, and with him his sons, and his servants, and many an armed man ; and he cried to Cepheus—

" You shall not marry your daughter to this stranger, of whom no one knows even the name. Was not Andromeda betrothed to my son ? And now she is safe again, has he not a right to claim her ? "

But Perseus laughed, and answered, " If your son is in want of a bride, let him save a maiden for himself. As yet he seems but a helpless bridegroom. He left this one to die, and dead she is to him. I saved her alive, and alive she is to me, but to no one else. Ungrateful man ! have I not saved your land, and the lives of your sons and daughters, and will you requite me thus ? Go, or it will be worse for you." But all the men-at-arms drew their swords, and rushed on him like wild beasts.

Then he unveiled the Gorgon's head, and said, " This has delivered my bride from one wild beast : it shall deliver her from many."

And as he spoke Phineus and all his men-at-
arms stopped short, and stiffened each man as
he stood ; and before Perseus had drawn the
goat-skin over the face again, they were all
turned into stone.

Then Perseus bade the people bring levers
and roll them out ; and what was done with
them after that I cannot tell.

So they made a great wedding-feast, which
lasted seven whole days, and who so happy as
Perseus and Andromeda ?

But on the eighth night Perseus dreamed a
dream ; and he saw standing beside him Pallas
Athené, as he had seen her in Seriphos seven
long years before ; and she stood and called
him by name, and said—

" Perseus, you have played the man, and see,
you have your reward. Know now that the
Gods are just, and help him who helps himself.
Now give me here Herpé the sword, and the
sandals, and the hat of darkness, that I may
give them back to their owners ; but the Gorgon's head you shall keep a while, for you will
need it in your land of Greece. Then you shall
lay it up in my temple at Seriphos, that I may
wear it on my shield for ever, a terror to the

Titans and the monsters, and the foes of Gods
and men. And as for this land, I have appeased the sea and the fire, and there shall be
no more floods nor earthquakes. But let the
people build altars to Father Zeus, and to me,
and worship the Immortals, the Lords of heaven
and earth."

And Perseus rose to give her the sword, and
the cap, and the sandals; but he woke, and his
dream vanished away. And yet it was not
altogether a dream; for the goat-skin with the
head was in its place; but the sword, and the
cap, and the sandals were gone, and Perseus
never saw them more.

Then a great awe fell on Perseus; and he
went out in the morning to the people, and told
his dream, and bade them build altars to Zeus,
the Father of Gods and men, and to Athené, who
gives wisdom to heroes; and fear no more the
earthquakes and the floods, but sow and build
in peace. And they did so for a while and
prospered; but after Perseus was gone they forgot Zeus and Athené, and worshipped again
Atergatis the queen, and the undying fish of
the sacred lake, where Deucalion's deluge was
swallowed up, and they burnt their children

before the Fire King, till Zeus was angry with that foolish people, and brought a strange nation against them out of Egypt, who fought against them and wasted them utterly, and dwelt in their cities for many a hundred years.

PART V

HOW PERSEUS CAME HOME AGAIN

AND when a year was ended Perseus hired
Phœnicians from Tyre, and cut down
cedars, and built himself a noble galley; and
painted its cheeks with vermilion, and pitched
its sides with pitch; and in it he put Andromeda, and all her dowry of jewels, and rich
shawls, and spices from the East; and great
was the weeping when they rowed away. But
the remembrance of his brave deed was left
behind; and Andromeda's rock was shown at
Iopa in Palestine till more than a thousand
years were past.

So Perseus and the Phœnicians rowed to the
westward, across the sea of Crete, till they came
to the blue Ægean and the pleasant Isles of
Hellas, and Seriphos, his ancient home.

Then he left his galley on the beach, and
went up as of old; and he embraced his mother,

and Dictys his good foster-father, and they wept over each other a long while, for it was seven years and more since they had met.

Then Perseus went out, and up to the hall of Polydectes; and underneath the goat-skin he bore the Gorgon's head.

And when he came into the hall, Polydectes sat at the table-head, and all his nobles and landowners on either side, each according to his rank, feasting on the fish and the goat's flesh, and drinking the blood-red wine. The harpers harped, and the revellers shouted, and the wine-cups rang merrily as they passed from hand to hand, and great was the noise in the hall of Polydectes.

Then Perseus stood upon the threshold, and called to the king by name. But none of the guests knew Perseus, for he was changed by his long journey. He had gone out a boy, and he was come home a hero; his eye shone like an eagle's, and his beard was like a lion's beard, and he stood up like a wild bull in his pride.

But Polydectes the wicked knew him, and hardened his heart still more; and scornfully he called—

"Ah, foundling! have you found it more easy to promise than to fulfil?"

"Those whom the Gods help fulfil their promises; and those who despise them reap as they have sown. Behold the Gorgon's head!"

Then Perseus drew back the goat-skin, and held aloft the Gorgon's head.

Pale grew Polydectes and his guests as they looked upon that dreadful face. They tried to rise up from their seats: but from their seats they never rose, but stiffened, each man where he sat, into a ring of cold gray stones.

Then Perseus turned and left them, and went down to his galley in the bay; and he gave the kingdom to good Dictys, and sailed away with his mother and his bride.

And Polydectes and his guests sat still, with the wine-cups before them on the board, till the rafters crumbled down above their heads, and the walls behind their backs, and the table crumbled down between them, and the grass sprung up about their feet: but Polydectes and his guests sit on the hillside, a ring of gray stones until this day.

But Perseus rowed westward toward Argos, and landed, and went up to the town. And

when he came, he found that Acrisius his
grandfather had fled. For Prœtus his wicked
brother had made war against him afresh, and
had come across the river from Tiryns, and
conquered Argos, and Acrisius had fled to
Larissa, in the country of the wild Pelasgi.

Then Perseus called the Argives together,
and told them who he was, and all the noble
deeds which he had done. And all the nobles
and the yeomen made him king, for they saw
that he had a royal heart ; and they fought
with him against Argos, and took it, and killed
Prœtus, and made the Cyclopes serve them,
and build them walls round Argos, like the
walls which they had built at Tiryns ; and there
were great rejoicings in the vale of Argos, because they had got a king from Father Zeus.

But Perseus' heart yearned after his grandfather, and he said, " Surely he is my flesh and
blood, and he will love me now that I am come
home with honour : I will go and find him, and
bring him home, and we will reign together in
peace."

So Perseus sailed away with his Phœnicians,
round Hydrea and Sunium, past Marathon and
the Attic shore, and through Euripus, and up

F

the long Eubœan sea, till he came to the town of Larissa, where the wild Pelasgi dwelt.

And when he came there, all the people were in the fields, and there was feasting, and all kinds of games; for Teutamenes their king wished to honour Acrisius, because he was the king of a mighty land.

So Perseus did not tell his name, but went up to the games unknown; for he said, " If I carry away the prize in the games, my grand-father's heart will be softened toward me."

So he threw off his helmet, and his cuirass, and all his clothes, and stood among the youths of Larissa, while all wondered at him, and said, " Who is this young stranger, who stands like a wild bull in his pride ? Surely he is one of the heroes, the sons of the Immortals, from Olympus."

And when the games began, they wondered yet more; for Perseus was the best man of all at running, and leaping, and wrestling, and throwing the javelin ; and he won four crowns, and took them, and then he said to himself, " There is a fifth crown yet to be won : I will win that, and lay them all upon the knees of my grandfather."

And as he spoke, he saw where Acrisius sat,

by the side of Teutamenes the king, with his white beard flowing down upon his knees, and his royal staff in his hand; and Perseus wept when he looked at him, for his heart yearned after his kin; and he said, "Surely he is a kingly old man, yet he need not be ashamed of his grandson."

Then he took the quoits, and hurled them five fathoms beyond all the rest; and the people shouted, "Further yet, brave stranger! There has never been such a hurler in this land."

Then Perseus put out all his strength and hurled. But a gust of wind came from the sea, and carried the quoit aside, and far beyond all the rest; and it fell on the foot of Acrisius, and he swooned away with the pain.

Perseus shrieked, and ran up to him; but when they lifted the old man up he was dead, for his life was slow and feeble.

Then Perseus rent his clothes, and cast dust upon his head, and wept a long while for his grandfather. At last he rose, and called to all the people aloud, and said—

"The Gods are true, and what they have ordained must be. I am Perseus, the grandson of this dead man, the far-famed slayer of the Gorgon."

Then he told them how the prophecy had declared that he should kill his grandfather, and all the story of his life.

So they made a great mourning for Acrisius, and burnt him on a right rich pile; and Perseus went to the temple, and was purified from the guilt of the death, because he had done it unknowingly.

Then he went home to Argos, and reigned there well with fair Andromeda; and they had four sons and three daughters, and died in a good old age.

And when they died, the ancients say, Athené took them up into the sky, with Cepheus and Cassiopœia. And there on starlight nights you may see them shining still; Cepheus with his kingly crown, and Cassiopœia in her ivory chair, plaiting her star-spangled tresses, and Perseus with the Gorgon's head, and fair Andromeda beside him, spreading her long white arms across the heaven, as she stood when chained to the stone for the monster. All night long they shine, for a beacon to wandering sailors; but all day they feast with the Gods, on the still blue peaks of Olympus.

Story II.—The Argonauts

PART I

HOW THE CENTAUR TRAINED THE HEROES ON PELION

I HAVE told you of a hero who fought with wild beasts and with wild men ; but now I have a tale of heroes who sailed away into a distant land, to win themselves renown for ever, in the adventure of the Golden Fleece.

Whither they sailed, my children, I cannot clearly tell. It all happened long ago ; so long that it has all grown dim, like a dream which you dreamt last year. And why they went I cannot tell : some say that it was to win gold. It may be so ; but the noblest deeds which have been done on earth have not been done for gold. It was not for the sake of gold that the Lord came down and died, and the Apostles went out to preach the good news in all lands.   The Spartans looked for no reward in money when they fought and died at Thermopylæ ; and Socrates the wise asked no pay from his countrymen, but lived poor and barefoot all his days, only caring to make men good.   And there are heroes in our days also, who do noble deeds, but not for gold.   Our discoverers did not go to make themselves rich when they sailed out one after another into the dreary frozen seas ; nor did the ladies who went out last year to drudge in the hospitals of the East, making themselves poor, that they might be rich in noble works.   And young men, too, whom you know, children, and some of them of your own kin, did they say to themselves, " How much money shall I earn ? " when they went out to the war, leaving wealth, and comfort, and a pleasant home, and all that money can give, to face hunger and thirst, and wounds and death, that they might fight for their country and their Queen ?   No, children, there is a better thing on earth than wealth, a better thing than life itself ; and that is, to have done something before you die, for which good men may honour you, and God your Father smile upon your work.

Therefore we will believe—why should we not ?—of these same Argonauts of old, that they too were noble men, who planned and did a noble deed ; and that therefore their fame has lived, and been told in story and in song, mixed up, no doubt, with dreams and fables, and yet true and right at heart. So we will honour these old Argonauts, and listen to their story as it stands ; and we will try to be like them, each of us in our place ; for each of us has a Golden Fleece to seek, and a wild sea to sail over ere we reach it, and dragons to fight ere it be ours.

And what was that first Golden Fleece ? I do not know, nor care. The old Hellens said that it hung in Colchis, which we call the Circassian coast, nailed to a beech-tree in the war-God's wood ; and that it was the fleece of the wondrous ram who bore Phrixus and Helle across the Euxine sea. For Phrixus and Helle were the children of the cloud-nymph, and of Athamas the Minuan king. And when a famine came upon the land, their cruel step-mother Ino wished to kill them, that her own children might reign, and said that they must be

sacrificed on an altar, to turn away the anger
of the Gods. So the poor children were
brought to the altar, and the priest stood ready
with his knife, when out of the clouds came
the Golden Ram, and took them on his back,
and vanished. Then madness came upon that
foolish king, Athamas, and ruin upon Ino and
her children. For Athamas killed one of them
in his fury, and Ino fled from him with the
other in her arms, and leaped from a cliff into
the sea, and was changed into a dolphin, such
as you have seen, which wanders over the
waves for ever sighing, with its little one
clasped to its breast.

But the people drove out King Athamas,
because he had killed his child; and he roamed
about in his misery, till he came to the Oracle
in Delphi. And the Oracle told him that he
must wander for his sin, till the wild beasts
should feast him as their guest. So he went
on in hunger and sorrow for many a weary
day, till he saw a pack of wolves. The wolves
were tearing a sheep; but when they saw
Athamas they fled, and left the sheep for him,
and he ate of it; and then he knew that the
oracle was fulfilled at last. So he wandered no

more ; but settled, and built a town, and became a king again.

But the ram carried the two children far away over land and sea, till he came to the Thracian Chersonese, and there Helle fell into the sea. So those narrow straits are called "Hellespont," after her; and they bear that name until this day.

Then the ram flew on with Phrixus to the north-east across the sea which we call the Black Sea now ; but the Hellens call it Euxine. And at last, they say, he stopped at Colchis, on the steep Circassian coast; and there Phrixus married Chalciope, the daughter of Aietes the king; and offered the ram in sacrifice ; and Aietes nailed the ram's fleece to a beech, in the grove of Ares the war-God.

And after awhile Phrixus died, and was buried, but his spirit had no rest ; for he was buried far from his native land, and the pleasant hills of Hellas. So he came in dreams to the heroes of the Minuai, and called sadly by their beds, " Come and set my spirit free, that I may go home to my fathers and to my kinsfolk, and the pleasant Minuan land."

And they asked, " How shall we set your spirit free ? "

"You must sail over the sea to Colchis, and bring home the golden fleece; and then my spirit will come back with it, and I shall sleep with my fathers and have rest."

He came thus, and called to them often; but when they woke they looked at each other, and said, "Who dare sail to Colchis, or bring home the golden fleece?" And in all the country none was brave enough to try it; for the man and the time were not come.

Phrixus had a cousin called Æson, who was king in Iolcos by the sea. There he ruled over the rich Minuan heroes, as Athamas his uncle ruled in Bœotia; and, like Athamas, he was an unhappy man. For he had a step-brother named Pelias, of whom some said that he was a nymph's son, and there were dark and sad tales about his birth. When he was a babe he was cast out on the mountains, and a wild mare came by and kicked him. But a shepherd passing found the baby, with its face all blackened by the blow; and took him home, and called him Pelias, because his face was bruised and black. And he grew up fierce and lawless, and did many a fearful deed; and at last he drove out Æson his step-brother, and then his own brother Neleus, and took the kingdom to himself, and ruled over the rich Minuan heroes, in Iolcos by the sea.

And Æson, when he was driven out, went sadly away out of the town, leading his little son by the hand; and he said to himself, " I must hide the child in the mountains; or Pelias will surely kill him, because he is the heir."

So he went up from the sea across the valley, through the vineyards and the olive groves, and across the torrent of Anauros, toward Pelion the ancient mountain, whose brows are white with snow.

He went up and up into the mountain, over marsh, and crag, and down, till the boy was tired and footsore, and Æson had to bear him in his arms, till he came to the mouth of a lonely cave, at the foot of a mighty cliff.

Above the cliff the snow-wreaths hung, dripping and cracking in the sun ; but at its foot around the cave's mouth grew all fair flowers and herbs, as if in a garden, ranged in order, each sort by itself. There they grew gaily in the sunshine, and the spray of the torrent from above ; while from the cave came the sound of music, and a man's voice singing to the harp.

Then Æson put down the lad, and whispered—

"Fear not, but go in, and whomsoever you shall find, lay your hands upon his knees, and say, 'In the name of Zeus, the father of Gods and men, I am your guest from this day forth."

Then the lad went in without trembling, for he too was a hero's son; but when he was within, he stopped in wonder to listen to that magic song.

And there he saw the singer lying upon bearskins and fragrant boughs: Cheiron, the ancient centaur, the wisest of all things beneath the sky. Down to the waist he was a man, but below he was a noble horse; his white hair rolled down over his broad shoulders, and his white beard over his broad brown chest; and his eyes were wise and mild, and his forehead like a mountain-wall.

And in his hands he held a harp of gold, and struck it with a golden key; and as he struck, he sang till his eyes glittered, and filled all the cave with light.

And he sang of the birth of Time, and of the heavens and the dancing stars; and of the ocean, and the ether, and the fire, and the

shaping of the wondrous earth. And he sang
of the treasures of the hills, and the hidden
jewels of the mine, and the veins of fire and
metal, and the virtues of all healing herbs, and
of the speech of birds, and of prophecy, and of
hidden things to come.

Then he sang of health, and strength, and
manhood, and a valiant heart; and of music,
and hunting, and wrestling, and all the games
which heroes love ; and of travel, and wars,
and sieges, and a noble death in fight ; and
then he sang of peace and plenty, and of equal
justice in the land ; and as he sang the boy
listened wide-eyed, and forgot his errand in the
song.

And at the last old Cheiron was silent, and
called the lad with a soft voice.

And the lad ran trembling to him, and
would have laid his hands upon his knees ; but
Cheiron smiled, and said, "Call hither your
father Æson, for I know you, and all that has
befallen, and saw you both afar in the valley,
even before you left the town."

Then Æson came in sadly, and Cheiron
asked him, "Why camest you not yourself to
me, Æson the Æolid ? "

And Æson said—

" I thought, Cheiron will pity the lad if he sees him come alone; and I wished to try whether he was fearless, and dare venture like a hero's son. But now I entreat you by Father Zeus, let the boy be your guest till better times, and train him among the sons of the heroes, that he may avenge his father's house."

Then Cheiron smiled, and drew the lad to him, and laid his hand upon his golden locks, and said, " Are you afraid of my horse's hoofs, fair boy, or will you be my pupil from this day ?"

" I would gladly have horse's hoofs like you, if I could sing such songs as yours."

And Cheiron laughed, and said, " Sit here by me till sundown, when your playfellows will come home, and you shall learn like them to be a king, worthy to rule over gallant men."

Then he turned to Æson, and said, " Go back in peace, and bend before the storm like a prudent man. This boy shall not cross the Anauros again, till he has become a glory to you and to the house of Æolus."

And Æson wept over his son and went away; but the boy did not weep, so full was his fancy of that strange cave, and the centaur, and his song, and the playfellows whom he was to see.

Then Cheiron put the lyre into his hands, and taught him how to play it, till the sun sank low behind the cliff, and a shout was heard outside.

And then in came the sons of the heroes, Æneas, and Heracles, and Peleus, and many another mighty name.

And great Cheiron leapt up joyfully, and his hoofs made the cave resound, as they shouted, "Come out, Father Cheiron; come out and see our game." And one cried, "I have killed two deer;" and another, "I took a wild cat among the crags;" and Heracles dragged a wild goat after him by its horns, for he was as huge as a mountain crag; and Cœneus carried a bear-cub under each arm, and laughed when they scratched and bit, for neither tooth nor steel could wound him.

And Cheiron praised them all, each according to his deserts.

Only one walked apart and silent, Asclepius, the too-wise child, with his bosom full of herbs and flowers, and round his wrist a spotted snake; he came with downcast eyes to Cheiron, and whispered how he had watched the snake cast its old skin, and grow young again before his eyes, and how he had gone down into a village in the vale, and cured a dying man with a herb which he had seen a sick goat eat.

And Cheiron smiled, and said, " To each Athené and Apollo give some gift, and each is worthy in his place ; but to this child they have given an honour beyond all honours, to cure while others kill."

Then the lads brought in wood, and split it, and lighted a blazing fire ; and others skinned the deer and quartered them, and set them to roast before the fire ; and while the venison was cooking they bathed in the snow-torrent, and washed away the dust and sweat.

And then all ate till they could eat no more (for they had tasted nothing since the dawn), and drank of the clear spring water, for wine is not fit for growing lads. And when the remnants were put away, they all lay down upon the skins and leaves about the fire, and each took the lyre in turn, and sang and played with all his heart.

And after a while they all went out to a plot of grass at the cave's mouth, and there they boxed, and ran, and wrestled, and laughed till the stones fell from the cliffs.

Then Cheiron took his lyre, and all the lads joined hands; and as he played, they danced to his measure, in and out, and round and round. There they danced hand in hand, till the night fell over land and sea, while the black glen shone with their broad white limbs and the gleam of their golden hair.

And the lad danced with them, delighted, and then slept a wholesome sleep, upon fragrant leaves of bay, and myrtle, and marjoram, and flowers of thyme; and rose at the dawn, and bathed in the torrent, and became a school-fellow to the heroes' sons, and forgot Iolcos, and his father, and all his former life. But he grew strong, and brave, and cunning, upon the pleasant downs of Pelion, in the keen, hungry mountain air. And he learnt to wrestle, and to box, and to hunt, and to play upon the harp; and next he learnt to ride, for old Cheiron used to mount him on his back; and he learnt the virtues of all herbs, and how to cure all wounds; and Cheiron called him Jason the healer, and that is his name until this day.

G

PART II

HOW JASON LOST HIS SANDAL IN ANAUROS

AND ten years came and went, and Jason was grown to be a mighty man. Some of his fellows were gone, and some were growing up by his side. Asclepius was gone into Peloponnese to work his wondrous cures on men; and some say he used to raise the dead to life. And Heracles was gone to Thebes to fulfil those famous labours which have become a proverb among men. And Peleus had married a sea-nymph, and his wedding is famous to this day. And Æneas was gone home to Troy, and many a noble tale you will read of him, and of all the other gallant heroes, the scholars of Cheiron the just. And it happened on a day that Jason stood on the mountain, and looked north and south and east and west; and Cheiron stood by him and watched him, for he knew that the time was come.

And Jason looked and saw the plains of Thessaly, where the Lapithai breed their horses ; and the lake of Boibé, and the stream which runs northward to Peneus and Tempe ; and he looked north, and saw the mountain wall which guards the Magnesian shore ; Olympus, the seat of the Immortals, and Ossa, and Pelion, where he stood. Then he looked east and saw the bright blue sea, which stretched away for ever toward the dawn. Then he looked south, and saw a pleasant land, with white - walled towns and farms, nestling along the shore of a land-locked bay, while the smoke rose blue among the trees ; and he knew it for the bay of Pagasai, and the rich lowlands of Hæmonia, and Iolcos by the sea.

Then he sighed, and asked, " Is it true what the heroes tell me—that I am heir of that fair land ? "

" And what good would it be to you, Jason, if you were heir of that fair land ? "

" I would take it and keep it."

" A strong man has taken it and kept it long. Are you stronger than Pelias the ter-rible ? "

" I can try my strength with his," said Jason ; but Cheiron sighed, and said—

" You have many a danger to go through before you rule in Iolcos by the sea ; many a danger and many a woe ; and strange troubles in strange lands, such as man never saw before."

" The happier I," said Jason, "to see what man never saw before."

And Cheiron sighed again, and said, " The eaglet must leave the nest when it is fledged. Will you go to Iolcos by the sea ? Then promise me two things before you go."

Jason promised, and Cheiron answered, " Speak harshly to no soul whom you may meet, and stand by the word which you shall speak."

Jason wondered why Cheiron asked this of him ; but he knew that the Centaur was a prophet, and saw things long before they came. So he promised, and leapt down the mountain, to take his fortune like a man.

He went down through the arbutus thickets, and across the downs of thyme, till he came to the vineyard walls, and the pomegranates and the olives in the glen ; and among the olives roared Anauros, all foaming with a summer flood.

And on the bank of Anauros sat a woman, all wrinkled, gray, and old ; her head shook palsied on her breast, and her hands shook palsied on her knees; and when she saw Jason, she spoke whining, " Who will carry me across the flood ? "

Jason was bold and hasty, and was just going to leap into the flood : and yet he thought twice before he leapt, so loud roared the torrent down, all brown from the mountain rains, and silver-veined with melting snow ; while underneath he could hear the boulders rumbling like the tramp of horsemen or the roll of wheels, as they ground along the narrow channel, and shook the rocks on which he stood.

But the old woman whined all the more, " I am weak and old, fair youth. For Hera's sake, carry me over the torrent."

And Jason was going to answer her scornfully, when Cheiron's words came to his mind.

So he said, " For Hera's sake, the Queen of the Immortals on Olympus, I will carry you over the torrent, unless we both are drowned midway."

Then the old dame leapt upon his back, as nimbly as a goat; and Jason staggered in, wondering; and the first step was up to his knees.

The first step was up to his knees, and the second step was up to his waist; and the stones rolled about his feet, and his feet slipped about the stones; so he went on staggering and panting, while the old woman cried from off his back—

"Fool, you have wet my mantle! Do you make game of poor old souls like me?"

Jason had half a mind to drop her, and let her get through the torrent by herself; but Cheiron's words were in his mind, and he said only, "Patience, mother; the best horse may stumble some day."

At last he staggered to the shore, and set her down upon the bank; and a strong man he needed to have been, or that wild water he never would have crossed.

He lay panting awhile upon the bank, and then leapt up to go upon his journey; but he cast one look at the old woman, for he thought, "She should thank me once at least."

And as he looked, she grew fairer than

all women, and taller than all men on earth;
and her garments shone like the summer sea,
and her jewels like the stars of heaven; and
over her forehead was a veil, woven of the
golden clouds of sunset; and through the veil
she looked down on him, with great soft
heifer's eyes; with great eyes, mild and awful,
which filled all the glen with light.

And Jason fell upon his knees, and hid
his face between his hands.

And she spoke, " I am the Queen of
Olympus, Hera the wife of Zeus. As thou
hast done to me, so will I do to thee. Call
on me in the hour of need, and try if the
Immortals can forget."

And when Jason looked up, she rose from
off the earth, like a pillar of tall white cloud,
and floated away across the mountain peaks,
toward Olympus the holy hill.

Then a great fear fell on Jason : but after
a while he grew light of heart ; and he blessed
old Cheiron, and said, " Surely the Centaur
is a prophet, and guessed what would come
to pass, when he bade me speak harshly to
no soul whom I might meet."

Then he went down toward Iolcos ; and

as he walked he found that he had lost one of his sandals in the flood.

And as he went through the streets, the people came out to look at him, so tall and fair was he; but some of the elders whispered together; and at last one of them stopped Jason, and called to him, "Fair lad, who are you, and whence come you; and what is your errand in the town?"

"My name, good father, is Jason, and I come from Pelion up above; and my errand is to Pelias your king; tell me then where his palace is."

But the old man started, and grew pale, and said, "Do you not know the oracle, my son, that you go so boldly through the town with but one sandal on?"

"I am a stranger here, and know of no oracle; but what of my one sandal? I lost the other in Anauros, while I was struggling with the flood."

Then the old man looked back to his companions; and one sighed, and another smiled; at last he said, "I will tell you, lest you rush upon your ruin unawares. The oracle in Delphi has said that a man wearing

one sandal should take the kingdom from
Pelias, and keep it for himself. Therefore
beware how you go up to his palace, for he
is the fiercest and most cunning of all kings."

Then Jason laughed a great laugh, like
a war-horse in his pride. " Good news, good
father, both for you and me. For that very
end I came into the town."

Then he strode on toward the palace of
Pelias, while all the people wondered at his
bearing.

And he stood in the doorway and cried,
" Come out, come out, Pelias the valiant, and
fight for your kingdom like a man."

Pelias came out wondering, and " Who are
you, bold youth ? " he cried.

" I am Jason, the son of Æson, the heir
of all this land."

Then Pelias lifted up his hands and eyes,
and wept, or seemed to weep ; and blessed
the heavens which had brought his nephew
to him, never to leave him more. " For," said
he, "I have but three daughters, and no son
to be my heir. You shall be my heir then,
and rule the kingdom after me, and marry
whichsoever of my daughters you shall choose;

though a sad kingdom you will find it, and whosoever rules it a miserable man. But come in, come in, and feast."

So he drew Jason in, whether he would or not, and spoke to him so lovingly and feasted him so well, that Jason's anger passed ; and after supper his three cousins came into the hall, and Jason thought that he should like well enough to have one of them for his wife.

But at last he said to Pelias, " Why do you look so sad, my uncle ? And what did you mean just now when you said that this was a doleful kingdom, and its ruler a miserable man ? "

Then Pelias sighed heavily again and again and again, like a man who had to tell some dreadful story, and was afraid to begin ; but at last—

" For seven long years and more have I never known a quiet night ; and no more will he who comes after me, till the golden fleece be brought home."

Then he told Jason the story of Phrixus, and of the golden fleece ; and told him, too, which was a lie, that Phrixus' spirit tormented him, calling to him day and night. And his daughters came, and told the same tale (for their father had taught them their parts), and wept, and said, " Oh who will bring home the golden fleece, that our uncle's spirit may rest : and that we may have rest also, whom he never lets sleep in peace ? "

Jason sat awhile, sad and silent; for he had often heard of that golden fleece ; but he looked on it as a thing hopeless and impossible for any mortal man to win it.

But when Pelias saw him silent, he began to talk of other things, and courted Jason more and more, speaking to him as if he was certain to be his heir, and asking his advice about the kingdom ; till Jason, who was young and simple, could not help saying to himself, " Surely he is not the dark man whom people call him. Yet why did he drive my father out ? " And he asked Pelias boldly, " Men say that you are terrible, and a man of blood ; but I find you a kind and hospitable man ; and as you are to me, so will I be to you. Yet why did you drive my father out ? "

Pelias smiled, and sighed. " Men have slandered me in that, as in all things. Your father was growing old and weary, and he gave the kingdom up to me of his own will. You shall see him to-morrow, and ask him; and he will tell you the same."

Jason's heart leapt in him when he heard that he was to see his father; and he believed all that Pelias said, forgetting that his father might not dare to tell the truth.

"One thing more there is," said Pelias, "on which I need your advice; for, though you are young, I see in you a wisdom beyond your years. There is one neighbour of mine, whom I dread more than all men on earth. I am stronger than he now, and can command him; but I know that if he stay among us, he will work my ruin in the end. Can you give me a plan, Jason, by which I can rid myself of that man?"

After awhile Jason answered, half laughing, "Were I you, I would send him to fetch that same golden fleece; for if he once set forth after it you would never be troubled with him more."

And at that a bitter smile came across Pelias' lips, and a flash of wicked joy into his eyes; and Jason saw it, and started; and over his mind came the warning of the old man, and his own one sandal, and the oracle, and he saw that he was taken in a trap.

But Pelias only answered gently, " My son, he shall be sent forthwith."

"You mean me?" cried Jason, starting up, "because I came here with one sandal?" And he lifted his fist angrily, while Pelias stood up to him like a wolf at bay; and whether of the two was the stronger and the fiercer it would be hard to tell.

But after a moment Pelias spoke gently, " Why then so rash, my son? You, and not I, have said what is said; why blame me for what I have not done? Had you bid me love the man of whom I spoke, and made him my son-in-law and heir, I would have obeyed you; and what if I obey you now, and send the man to win himself immortal fame? I have not harmed you, or him. One thing at least I know, that he will go, and that gladly; for he has a hero's heart within him, loving glory, and scorning to break the word which he has given."

Jason saw that he was entrapped; but his second promise to Cheiron came into his mind, and he thought, " What if the Centaur were a prophet in that also, and meant that I should win the fleece!" Then he cried aloud—

"You have well spoken, cunning uncle of mine! I love glory, and I dare keep to my word. I will go and fetch this golden fleece. Promise me but this in return, and keep your word as I keep mine. Treat my father lovingly while I am gone, for the sake of the all-seeing Zeus; and give me up the kingdom for my own on the day that I bring back the golden fleece."

Then Pelias looked at him and almost loved him, in the midst of all his hate; and said, "I promise, and I will perform. It will be no shame to give up my kingdom to the man who wins that fleece."

Then they swore a great oath between them; and afterwards both went in, and lay down to sleep.

But Jason could not sleep for thinking of his mighty oath, and how he was to fulfil it, all alone, and without wealth or friends. So he tossed a long time upon his bed, and thought of this plan and of that; and sometimes Phrixus seemed to call him, in a thin voice, faint and low, as if it came from far across the sea, "Let me come home to my fathers and have rest." And sometimes he seemed to see the eyes of Hera, and to hear her words again—"Call on me in the hour of need, and see if the Immortals can forget."

And on the morrow he went to Pelias, and said, "Give me a victim, that I may sacrifice to Hera." So he went up, and offered his sacrifice; and as he stood by the altar Hera sent a thought into his mind; and he went back to Pelias, and said—

"If you are indeed in earnest, give me two heralds, that they may go round to all the princes of the Minuai, who were pupils of the Centaur with me, that we may fit out a ship together, and take what shall befall."

At that Pelias praised his wisdom, and hastened to send the heralds out; for he said in his heart, "Let all the princes go with him, and, like him, never return; for so I shall be lord of all the Minuai, and the greatest king in Hellas."

PART III

SO the heralds went out, and cried to all the heroes of the Minuai, "Who dare come to the adventure of the golden fleece?"

And Hera stirred the hearts of all the princes, and they came from all their valleys to the yellow sands of Pagasai. And first came Heracles the mighty, with his lion's skin and club, and behind him Hylas his young squire, who bore his arrows and his bow; and Tiphys, the skilful steersman; and Butes, the fairest of all men; and Castor and Polydeuces the twins, the sons of the magic swan; and Cæneus, the strongest of mortals, whom the Centaurs tried in vain to kill, and overwhelmed him with trunks of pine-trees, but even so he would not die; and thither came Zetes and Calais, the winged sons of the north wind; and Peleus, the father of Achilles, whose bride was silver-footed Thetis, the goddess of the sea. And thither came Telamon and Oileus, the fathers of the two Aiantes, who fought upon the plains of Troy; and Mopsus, the wise soothsayer, who knew the speech of birds; and Idmon, to whom Phœbus gave a tongue to prophesy of things to come; and Ancaios, who could read the stars, and knew all the circles of the heavens; and Argus, the famed shipbuilder, and many a hero more, in helmets of brass and gold with tall dyed horse-hair crests, and embroidered shirts of linen beneath their coats of mail, and greaves of polished tin to guard their knees in fight; with each man his shield upon his shoulder, of many a fold of tough bull's hide, and his sword of tempered bronze in his silver-studded belt; and in his right hand a pair of lances, of the heavy white ash-staves.

So they came down to Iolcos, and all the city came out to meet them, and were never tired with looking at their height, and their beauty, and their gallant bearing, and the glitter of their inlaid arms. And some said, "Never was such a gathering of the heroes since the Hellens conquered the land." But the women sighed over them, and whispered, "Alas! they are all going to their death!"

H

Then they felled the pines on Pelion, and shaped them with the axe, and Argus taught them to build a galley, the first long ship which ever sailed the seas. They pierced her for fifty oars—an oar for each hero of the crew—and pitched her with coal-black pitch, and painted her bows with vermilion; and they named her *Argo* after Argus, and worked at her all day long. And at night Pelias feasted them like a king, and they slept in his palace-porch.

But Jason went away to the northward, and into the land of Thrace, till he found Orpheus, the prince of minstrels, where he dwelt in his cave under Rhodope, among the savage Cicon tribes. And he asked him, "Will you leave your mountains, Orpheus, my fellow-scholar in old times, and cross Strymon once more with me, to sail with the heroes of the Minuai, and bring home the golden fleece, and charm for us all men and all monsters with your magic harp and song?"

Then Orpheus sighed, "Have I not had enough of toil and of weary wandering far and wide since I lived in Cheiron's cave, above Iolcos by the sea? In vain is the skill and the voice which my goddess mother gave me; in vain have I sung and laboured; in vain I went down to the dead, and charmed all the kings of Hades, to win back Eurydice my bride. For I won her, my beloved, and lost her again the same day, and wandered away in my madness, even to Egypt and the Libyan sands, and the isles of all the seas, driven on by the terrible gadfly, while I charmed in vain the hearts of men, and the savage forest beasts, and the trees, and the lifeless stones, with my magic harp and song, giving rest, but finding none. But at last Calliope my mother delivered me, and brought me home in peace; and I dwell here in the cave alone, among the savage Cicon tribes, softening their wild hearts with music and the gentle laws of Zeus. And now I must go out again, to the ends of all the earth, far away into the misty darkness, to the last wave of the Eastern Sea. But what is doomed must be, and a friend's demand obeyed; for prayers are the daughters of Zeus, and who honours them honours him."

Then Orpheus rose up sighing, and took his harp, and went over Strymon. And he led Jason to the south-west, up the banks of Haliacmon and over the spurs of Pindus, to Dodona the town of Zeus, where it stood by the side of the sacred lake, and the fountain which breathed out fire, in the darkness of the ancient oakwood, beneath the mountain of the hundred springs. And he led him to the holy oak, where the black dove settled in old times, and was changed into the priestess of Zeus, and gave oracles to all nations round. And he bade him cut down a bough, and sacrifice to Hera and to Zeus; and they took the bough and came to Iolcos, and nailed it to the beak-head of the ship.

And at last the ship was finished, and they tried to launch her down the beach; but she was too heavy for them to move her, and her keel sank deep into the sand. Then all the heroes looked at each other blushing; but Jason spoke, and said, " Let us ask the magic bough; perhaps it can help us in our need."

Then a voice came from the bough, and Jason heard the words it said, and bade Orpheus play upon the harp, while the heroes waited round, holding the pine-trunk rollers, to help her toward the sea.

Then Orpheus took his harp, and began his magic song—" How sweet it is to ride upon the surges, and to leap from wave to wave, while the wind sings cheerful in the cordage, and the oars flash fast among the foam! How sweet it is to roam across the ocean, and see new towns and wondrous lands, and to come home laden with treasure, and to win undying fame!"

And the good ship *Argo* heard him, and longed to be away and out at sea; till she stirred in every timber, and heaved from stem to stern, and leapt up from the sand upon the rollers, and plunged onward like a gallant horse; and the heroes fed her path with pine-trunks, till she rushed into the whispering sea.

Then they stored her well with food and water, and pulled the ladder up on board, and settled themselves each man to his oar, and kept time to Orpheus' harp; and away across the bay they rowed southward, while the people lined the cliffs; and the women wept, while the men shouted, at the starting of that gallant crew.

PART IV

AND what happened next, my children, whether it be true or not, stands written in ancient songs, which you shall read for yourselves some day. And grand old songs they are, written in grand old rolling verse; and they call them the Songs of Orpheus, or the Orphics, to this day. And they tell how the heroes came to Aphetai, across the bay, and waited for the south-west wind, and chose themselves a captain from their crew: and how all called for Heracles, because he was the strongest and most huge; but Heracles refused, and called for Jason, because he was the wisest of them all. So Jason was chosen captain; and Orpheus heaped a pile of wood, and slew a bull, and offered it to Hera, and called all the heroes to stand round, each man's head crowned with olive, and to strike their swords into the bull. Then he filled a golden goblet with the bull's blood, and with wheaten flour, and honey, and wine, and the bitter salt-sea water, and bade the heroes taste. So each tasted the goblet, and passed it round, and vowed an awful vow : and they vowed before the sun, and the night, and the blue-haired sea who shakes the land, to stand by Jason faithfully in the adventure of the golden fleece ; and whosoever shrank back, or disobeyed, or turned traitor to his vow, then justice should minister against him, and the Erinnues who track guilty men.

Then Jason lighted the pile, and burnt the carcase of the bull ; and they went to their ship and sailed eastward, like men who have a work to do ; and the place from which they went was called Aphetai, the sailing-place, from that day forth. Three thousand years and more they sailed away, into the unknown Eastern seas ; and great nations have come and gone since then, and many a storm has swept the earth ; and many a mighty armament, to which *Argo* would be but one small boat ; English and French, Turkish and Russian, have sailed those waters since ; yet the fame of that small *Argo* lives for ever, and her name is become a proverb among men.

So they sailed past the Isle of Sciathos, with the Cape of Sepius on their left, and turned to the northward toward Pelion, up the long Magnesian shore. On their right hand was the open sea, and on their left old Pelion rose, while the clouds crawled round his dark pine-forests, and his caps of summer snow. And their hearts yearned for the dear old mountain, as they thought of pleasant days gone by, and of the sports of their boyhood, and their hunting, and their schooling in the cave beneath the cliff. And at last Peleus spoke, "Let us land here, friends, and climb the dear old hill once more. We are going on a fearful journey; who knows if we shall see Pelion again? Let us go up to Cheiron our master, and ask his blessing ere we start. And I have a boy, too, with him, whom he trains as he trained me once—the son whom Thetis brought me, the silver-footed lady of the sea, whom I caught in the cave, and tamed her, though she changed her shape seven times. For she changed, as I held her, into water, and to vapour, and to burning flame, and to a rock, and to a blackmaned lion, and to a tall and stately tree. But I held her and held her ever, till she took her own shape again, and led her to my father's house, and won her for my bride. And all the rulers of Olympus came to our wedding, and the heavens and the earth rejoiced together, when an Immortal wedded mortal man. And now let me see my son; for it is not often I shall see him upon earth: famous he will be, but short-lived, and die in the flower of youth."

So Tiphys the helmsman steered them to the shore under the crags of Pelion; and they went up through the dark pine forests towards the Centaur's cave.

And they came into the misty hall, beneath the snow-crowned crag; and saw the great Centaur lying, with his huge limbs spread upon the rock; and beside him stood Achilles, the child whom no steel could wound, and played upon his harp right sweetly, while Cheiron watched and smiled.

Then Cheiron leapt up and welcomed them, and kissed them every one, and set a feast before them of swine's flesh, and venison, and good wine; and young Achilles served them, and carried the golden goblet round. And after supper all the heroes clapped their hands, and called on Orpheus to sing; but he refused, and said, "How can I, who am the younger, sing before our ancient host?" So they called on Cheiron to sing, and Achilles brought him his harp; and he began a wondrous song; a famous story of old time, of the fight between the Centaurs and the Lapithai, which you may still see carved in stone.* He sang how his brothers came to ruin by their folly, when they were mad with wine; and how they and the heroes fought, with fists, and teeth, and the goblets from which they drank; and how they tore up the pine-trees in their fury, and hurled great crags of stone, while the mountains thundered with the battle, and the land was wasted far and wide; till the Lapithai drove them from their home in the rich Thessalian plains to the lonely glens of Pindus, leaving Cheiron all alone. And the heroes praised his song right heartily; for some of them had helped in that great fight.

Then Orpheus took the lyre, and sang of Chaos, and the making of the wondrous World,

* In the Elgin Marbles.

and how all things sprang from Love, who could not live alone in the Abyss. And as he sang, his voice rose from the cave, above the crags, and through the tree-tops, and the glens of oak and pine. And the trees bowed their heads when they heard it, and the gray rocks cracked and rang, and the forest beasts crept near to listen, and the birds forsook their nests and hovered round. And old Cheiron clapt his hands together, and beat his hoofs upon the ground, for wonder at that magic song.

Then Peleus kissed his boy, and wept over him, and they went down to the ship; and Cheiron came down with them, weeping, and kissed them one by one, and blest them, and promised to them great renown. And the heroes wept when they left him, till their great hearts could weep no more ; for he was. kind and just and pious, and wiser than all beasts and men. Then he went up to a cliff and prayed for them, that they might come home safe and well ; while the heroes rowed away, and watched him standing on his cliff above the sea, with his great hands raised towards heaven, and his white locks waving in the wind ; and they strained their eyes to watch him to the last, for they felt that they should look on him no more.

So they rowed on over the long swell of the sea, past Olympus, the seat of the Immortals, and past the wooded bays of Athos, and Samothrace the sacred isle ; and they came past Lemnos to the Hellespont, and through the narrow strait of Abydos, and so on into the Propontis, which we call Marmora now. And there they met with Cyzicus, ruling in Asia over the Dolions, who, the songs say, was the son of Æneas, of whom you will hear many a tale some day. For Homer tells us how he fought at Troy, and Virgil how he sailed away and founded Rome ; and men believed until late years that from him sprang our old British kings. Now Cyzicus, the songs say, welcomed the heroes, for his father had been one of Cheiron's scholars ; so he welcomed them, and feasted them, and stored their ship with corn and wine, and cloaks and rugs, the songs say, and shirts, of which no doubt they stood in need.

But at night, while they lay sleeping, came down on them terrible men, who lived with the bears in the mountains, like Titans or giants in shape ; for each of them had six arms, and they fought with young firs and pines. But Heracles killed them all before morn with his deadly poisoned arrows ; but among them, in the darkness, he slew Cyzicus the kindly prince.

Then they got to their ship and to their oars, and Tiphys bade them cast off the hawsers and go to sea. But as he spoke a whirlwind came, and spun the *Argo* round, and twisted the hawsers together, so that no man could loose them. Then Tiphys dropped the rudder from his hand, and cried, " This comes from the Gods above." But Jason went forward, and asked counsel of the magic bough.

Then the magic bough spoke, and answered, " This is because you have slain Cyzicus your friend. You must appease his soul, or you will never leave this shore."

Jason went back sadly, and told the heroes what he had heard. And they leapt on shore, and searched till dawn ; and at dawn they found the body, all rolled in dust and blood, among the corpses of those monstrous beasts. And they wept over their kind host, and laid him on a fair bed, and heaped a huge mound over him, and offered black sheep at his tomb, and Orpheus sang a magic song to him, that his spirit might have rest. And then they held games at the tomb, after the custom of those times, and Jason gave prizes to each winner. To Ancæus he gave a golden cup, for he wrestled best of all ; and to Heracles a silver one, for he was the strongest of all ; and to Castor, who rode best, a golden crest ; and Polydeuces the boxer had a rich carpet; and to Orpheus for his song a sandal with golden wings. But Jason himself was the best of all the archers, and the Minuai crowned him with an olive crown ; and so, the songs say, the soul of good Cyzicus was appeased, and the heroes went on their way in peace.

But when Cyzicus' wife heard that he was dead she died likewise of grief; and her tears became a fountain of clear water, which flows the whole year round.

Then they rowed away, the songs say, along the Mysian shore, and past the mouth of Rhindacus, till they found a pleasant bay, sheltered by the long ridges of Arganthus, and by high walls of basalt rock. And there they ran the ship ashore upon the yellow sand, and furled the sail, and took the mast down, and lashed it in its crutch. And next they let down the ladder, and went ashore to sport and rest.

And there Heracles went away into the woods, bow in hand, to hunt wild deer; and Hylas the fair boy slipt away after him, and followed him by stealth, until he lost himself among the glens, and sat down weary to rest himself by the side of a lake; and there the water nymphs came up to look at him, and loved him, and carried him down under the lake to be their playfellow, for ever happy and young. And Heracles sought for him in vain, shouting his name till all the mountains rang; but Hylas never heard him, far down under the sparkling lake. So while Heracles wandered searching for him, a fair breeze sprang up, and Heracles was nowhere to be found; and the *Argo* sailed away, and Heracles was left behind, and never saw the noble Phasian stream.

Then the Minuai came to a doleful land, where Amycus the giant ruled, and cared nothing for the laws of Zeus, but challenged all strangers to box with him, and those whom

he conquered he slew. But Polydeuces the
boxer struck him a harder blow than he ever
felt before, and slew him; and the Minuai
went on up the Bosphorus, till they came to
the city of Phineus, the fierce Bithynian king;
for Zetes and Calais bade Jason land there,
because they had a work to do.

And they went up from the shore toward
the city, through forests white with snow; and
Phineus came out to meet them with a lean
and woful face, and said, "Welcome, gallant
heroes, to the land of bitter blasts, the land of
cold and misery; yet I will feast you as best I
can." And he led them in, and set meat before them; but before they could put their
hands to their mouths, down came two fearful
monsters, the like of whom man never saw;
for they had the faces and the hair of fair
maidens, but the wings and claws of hawks;
and they snatched the meat from off the table,
and flew shrieking out above the roofs.

Then Phineus beat his breast and cried,
"These are the Harpies, whose names are
the Whirlwind and the Swift, the daughters
of Wonder and of the Amber-nymph, and they
rob us night and day. They carried off the

daughters of Pandareus, whom all the Gods had blest; for Aphrodite fed them on Olympus with honey and milk and wine; and Hera gave them beauty and wisdom, and Athené skill in all the arts; but when they came to their wedding, the Harpies snatched them both away, and gave them to be slaves to the Erinnues, and live in horror all their days. And now they haunt me, and my people, and the Bosphorus, with fearful storms; and sweep away our food from off our tables, so that we starve in spite of all our wealth."

Then up rose Zetes and Calais, the winged sons of the North-wind, and said, "Do you not know us, Phineus, and these wings which grow upon our backs?" And Phineus hid his face in terror; but he answered not a word.

"Because you have been a traitor, Phineus, the Harpies haunt you night and day. Where is Cleopatra, our sister, your wife, whom you keep in prison? and where are her two children, whom you blinded in your rage, at the bidding of an evil woman, and cast them out upon the rocks? Swear to us that you will right our sister, and cast out that wicked

I

woman ; and then we will free you from your plague, and drive the whirlwind maidens to the south ; but if not, we will put out your eyes, as you put out the eyes of your own sons."

Then Phineus swore an oath to them, and drove out the wicked woman ; and Jason took those two poor children, and cured their eyes with magic herbs.

But Zetes and Calais rose up sadly and said, "Farewell now, heroes all ; farewell, our dear companions, with whom we played on Pelion in old times ; for a fate is laid upon us, and our day is come at last, in which we must hunt the whirlwinds over land and sea for ever ; and if we catch them they die, and if not, we die ourselves."

At that all the heroes wept ; but the two young men sprang up, and aloft into the air after the Harpies, and the battle of the winds began.

The heroes trembled in silence as they heard the shrieking of the blasts ; while the palace rocked and all the city, and great stones were torn from the crags, and the forest pines were hurled earthward, north and south and east and west, and the Bosphorus boiled white with foam, and the clouds were dashed against the cliffs.

But at last the battle ended, and the Harpies fled screaming toward the south, and the sons of the North-wind rushed after them, and brought clear sunshine where they passed. For many a league they followed them, over all the isles of the Cyclades, and away to the south-west across Hellas, till they came to the Ionian Sea, and there they fell upon the Echinades, at the mouth of the Achelous; and those isles were called the Whirlwind Isles for many a hundred years. But what became of Zetes and Calais I know not, for the heroes never saw them again : and some say that Heracles met them, and quarrelled with them, and slew them with his arrows; and some say that they fell down from weariness and the heat of the summer sun, and that the Sun-god buried them among the Cyclades, in the pleasant Isle of Tenos; and for many hundred years their grave was shown there, and over it a pillar, which turned to every wind. But those dark storms and whirlwinds haunt the Bosphorus until this day.

But the Argonauts went eastward, and out

into the open sea, which we now call the Black Sea, but it was called the Euxine then. No Hellen had ever crossed it, and all feared that dreadful sea, and its rocks, and shoals, and fogs, and bitter freezing storms; and they told strange stories of it, some false and some half-true, how it stretched northward to the ends of the earth, and the sluggish Putrid Sea, and the everlasting night, and the regions of the dead. So the heroes trembled, for all their courage, as they came into that wild Black Sea, and saw it stretching out before them, without a shore, as far as eye could see.

And first Orpheus spoke, and warned them, "We shall come now to the wandering blue rocks; my mother warned me of them, Calliope, the immortal muse."

And soon they saw the blue rocks shining like spires and castles of gray glass, while an ice-cold wind blew from them and chilled all the heroes' hearts. And as they neared they could see them heaving, as they rolled upon the long sea-waves, crashing and grinding together, till the roar went up to heaven. The sea sprang up in spouts between them, and swept round them in white sheets of foam; but their heads swung nodding high in air, while the wind whistled shrill among the crags.

The heroes' hearts sank within them, and they lay upon their oars in fear; but Orpheus called to Tiphys the helmsman, "Between them we must pass; so look ahead for an opening, and be brave, for Hera is with us." But Tiphys the cunning helmsman stood silent, clenching his teeth, till he saw a heron come flying mast-high toward the rocks, and hover awhile before them, as if looking for a passage through. Then he cried, " Hera has sent us a pilot; let us follow the cunning bird."

Then the heron flapped to and fro a moment, till he saw a hidden gap, and into it he rushed like an arrow, while the heroes watched what would befall.

And the blue rocks clashed together as the bird fled swiftly through ; but they struck but a feather from his tail, and then rebounded apart at the shock.

Then Tiphys cheered the heroes, and they shouted ; and the oars bent like withes beneath their strokes as they rushed between those toppling ice-crags and the cold blue lips of death. And ere the rocks could meet again they had passed them, and were safe out in the open sea.

And after that they sailed on wearily along the Asian coast, by the Black Cape and Thyneis, where the hot stream of Thymbris falls into the sea, and Sangarius, whose waters float on the Euxine, till they came to Wolf the river, and to Wolf the kindly king. And there died two brave heroes, Idmon and Tiphys the wise helmsman : one died of an evil sickness, and one a wild boar slew. So the heroes heaped a mound above them, and set upon it an oar on high, and left them there to sleep together, on the far off Lycian shore. But Idas killed the boar, and avenged Tiphys; and Ancaios took the rudder and was helmsman, and steered them on toward the east.

And they went on past Sinope, and many a mighty river's mouth, and past many a barbarous tribe, and the cities of the Amazons, the warlike women of the East, till all night they heard the clank of anvils and the roar of furnace-blasts, and the forge-fires shone like sparks through the darkness in the mountain glens aloft; for they were come to the shores of the Chalybes, the smiths who never tire, but serve Ares the cruel War-god, forging weapons day and night.

And at day-dawn they looked eastward, and midway between the sea and the sky they saw white snow-peaks hanging, glittering sharp and bright above the clouds. And they knew that they were come to Caucasus, at the end of all the earth : Caucasus the highest of all mountains, the father of the rivers of the East. On his peak lies chained the Titan, while a vulture tears his heart ; and at his feet are piled dark forests round the magic Colchian land.

And they rowed three days to the eastward, while Caucasus rose higher hour by hour, till they saw the dark stream of Phasis rushing headlong to the sea, and, shining above the tree-tops, the golden roofs of King Aietes, the child of the Sun.

Then out spoke Ancaios the helmsman, " We are come to our goal at last, for there are the roofs of Aietes, and the woods where all poisons grow ; but who can tell us where among them is hid the golden fleece ? Many a toil must we bear ere we find it, and bring it home to Greece."

But Jason cheered the heroes, for his heart

was high and bold; and he said, "I will go alone up to Aietes, though he be the child of the Sun, and win him with soft words. Better so than to go altogether, and to come to blows at once." But the Minuai would not stay behind, so they rowed boldly up the stream.

And a dream came to Aietes, and filled his heart with fear. He thought he saw a shining star, which fell into his daughter's lap; and that Medeia his daughter took it gladly, and carried it to the river-side, and cast it in, and there the whirling river bore it down, and out into the Euxine Sea.

Then he leapt up in fear, and bade his servants bring his chariot, that he might go down to the river-side and appease the nymphs, and the heroes whose spirits haunt the bank. So he went down in his golden chariot, and his daughters by his side, Medeia the fair witch-maiden, and Chalciope, who had been Phrixus' wife, and behind him a crowd of servants and soldiers, for he was a rich and mighty prince.

And as he drove down by the reedy river he saw *Argo* sliding up beneath the bank, and many a hero in her, like Immortals for beauty and for strength, as their weapons glittered round them in the level morning sunlight, through the white mist of the stream. But Jason was the noblest of all ; for Hera, who loved him, gave him beauty and tallness and terrible manhood.

And when they came near together and looked into each other's eyes the heroes were awed before Aietes as he shone in his chariot, like his father the glorious Sun ; for his robes were of rich gold tissue, and the rays of his diadem flashed fire ; and in his hand he bore a jewelled sceptre, which glittered like the stars ; and sternly he looked at them under his brows, and sternly he spoke and loud—

"Who are you, and what want you here, that you come to the shore of Cutaia ? Do you take no account of my rule, nor of my people the Colchians who serve me, who never tired yet in the battle, and know well how to face an invader ?"

And the heroes sat silent awhile before the face of that ancient king. But Hera the awful goddess put courage into Jason's heart, and he rose and shouted loudly in answer, "We are no pirates nor lawless men. We come not to plunder and to ravage, or carry away slaves from your land ; but my uncle, the son of Poseidon, Pelias the Minuan king, he it is who has set me on a quest to bring home the golden fleece. And these too, my bold comrades, they are no nameless men; for some are the sons of Immortals, and some of heroes far renowned. And we too never tire in battle, and know well how to give blows and to take ; yet we wish to be guests at your table : it will be better so for both."

Then Aietes' rage rushed up like a whirlwind, and his eyes flashed fire as he heard ; but he crushed his anger down in his breast, and spoke mildly a cunning speech—

"If you will fight for the fleece with my Colchians, then many a man must die. But do you indeed expect to win from me the fleece in fight? So few you are that if you be worsted I can load your ship with your corpses. But if you will be ruled by me, you will find it better far to choose the best man among you, and let him fulfil the labours which I demand. Then I will give him the golden fleece for a prize and a glory to you all."

So saying, he turned his horses and drove back in silence to the town. And the Minuai sat silent with sorrow, and longed for Heracles and his strength ; for there was no facing the thousands of the Colchians and the fearful chance of war.

But Chalciope, Phrixus' widow, went weeping to the town ; for she remembered her Minuan husband, and all the pleasures of her youth, while she watched the fair faces of his kinsmen, and their long locks of golden hair. And she whispered to Medeia her sister, "Why should all these brave men die ? why does not my father give them up the fleece, that my husband's spirit may have rest ? "

And Medeia's heart pitied the heroes, and Jason most of all ; and she answered, "Our father is stern and terrible, and who can win the golden fleece ? " But Chalciope said, " These men are not like our men ; there is nothing which they cannot dare or do."

And Medeia thought of Jason and his brave countenance, and said, " If there was one among them who knew no fear, I could show him how to win the fleece."

So in the dusk of evening they went down to the river-side, Chalciope and Medeia the witch-maiden, and Argus, Phrixus' son. And

Argus the boy crept forward, among the beds of reeds, till he came where the heroes were sleeping, on the thwarts of the ship, beneath the bank, while Jason kept ward on shore, and leant upon his lance full of thought. And the boy came to Jason, and said—

" I am the son of Phrixus, your cousin; and Chalciope my mother waits for you, to talk about the golden fleece."

Then Jason went boldly with the boy, and found the two princesses standing; and when Chalciope saw him she wept, and took his hands, and cried—

"O cousin of my beloved, go home before you die!"

" It would be base to go home now, fair princess, and to have sailed all these seas in vain." Then both the princesses besought him; but Jason said, " It is too late."

" But you know not," said Medeia, " what he must do who would win the fleece. He must tame the two brazen-footed bulls, who breathe devouring flame; and with them he must plough ere nightfall four acres in the field of Ares; and he must sow them with serpents' teeth, of which each tooth springs up into an

armed man. Then he must fight with all those
warriors; and little will it profit him to conquer
them, for the fleece is guarded by a serpent,
more huge than any mountain pine; and over
his body you must step if you would reach the
golden fleece."

Then Jason laughed bitterly. "Unjustly is
that fleece kept here, and by an unjust and
lawless king; and unjustly shall I die in my
youth, for I will attempt it ere another sun be
set."

Then Medeia trembled, and said, "No
mortal man can reach that fleece unless I guide
him through. For round it, beyond the river,
is a wall full nine ells high, with lofty towers
and buttresses, and mighty gates of threefold
brass; and over the gates the wall is arched,
with golden battlements above. And over the
gateway sits Brimo, the wild witch-huntress of
the woods, brandishing a pine-torch in her
hands, while her mad hounds howl around.
No man dare meet her or look on her, but only
I her priestess, and she watches far and wide
lest any stranger should come near."

"No wall so high but it may be climbed at
last, and no wood so thick but it may be

crawled through; no serpent so wary but he may be charmed, or witch-queen so fierce but spells may soothe her; and I may yet win the golden fleece, if a wise maiden help bold men."

And he looked at Medeia cunningly, and held her with his glittering eye, till she blushed and trembled, and said—

"Who can face the fire of the bulls' breath, and fight ten thousand armed men?"

"He whom you help," said Jason, flattering her, "for your fame is spread over all the earth. Are you not the queen of all enchantresses, wiser even than your sister Circe, in her fairy island in the West?"

"Would that I were with my sister Circe in her fairy island in the West, far away from sore temptation and thoughts which tear the heart! But if it must be so—for why should you die?—I have an ointment here; I made it from the magic ice-flower which sprang from Prometheus' wound, above the clouds on Caucasus, in the dreary fields of snow. Anoint yourself with that, and you shall have in you seven men's strength; and anoint your shield with it, and neither fire nor sword can harm you. But what you begin you must end before sunset, for its virtue lasts only one day. And anoint your helmet with it before you sow the serpents' teeth; and when the sons of earth spring up, cast your helmet among their ranks, and the deadly crop of the War-god's field will mow itself, and perish."

Then Jason fell on his knees before her, and thanked her and kissed her hands; and she gave him the vase of ointment, and fled trembling through the reeds. And Jason told his comrades what had happened, and showed them the box of ointment; and all rejoiced but Idas, and he grew mad with envy.

And at sunrise Jason went and bathed, and anointed himself from head to foot, and his shield, and his helmet, and his weapons, and bade his comrades try the spell. So they tried to bend his lance, but it stood like an iron bar; and Idas in spite hewed at it with his sword, but the blade flew to splinters in his face. Then they hurled their lances at his shield, but the spear-points turned like lead; and Caineus tried to throw him, but he never stirred a foot; and Polydeuces struck him with his fist a blow which would have killed an ox, but Jason only smiled, and the heroes danced about him with delight ; and he leapt, and ran, and shouted in the joy of that enormous strength, till the sun rose, and it was time to go and to claim Aietes' promise.

So he sent up Telamon and Aithalides to tell Aietes that he was ready for the fight ; and they went up among the marble walls, and beneath the roofs of gold, and stood in Aietes' hall, while he grew pale with rage.

"Fulfil your promise to us, child of the blazing Sun Give us the serpents' teeth, and let loose the fiery bulls ; for we have found a champion among us who can win the golden fleece."

And Aietes bit his lips, for he fancied that they had fled away by night : but he could not go back from his promise ; so he gave them the serpents' teeth.

Then he called for his chariot and his horses, and sent heralds through all the town ; and all the people went out with him to the dreadful War-god's field.

And there Aietes sat upon his throne, with his warriors on each hand, thousands and tens of thousands, clothed from head to foot in steel chain-mail. And the people and the women crowded to every window and bank and wall; while the Minuai stood together, a mere handful in the midst of that great host.

And Chalciope was there and Argus, trembling, and Medeia, wrapped closely in her veil; but Aietes did not know that she was muttering cunning spells between her lips.

Then Jason cried, "Fulfil your promise, and let your fiery bulls come forth."

Then Aietes bade open the gates, and the magic bulls leapt out. Their brazen hoofs rang upon the ground, and their nostrils sent out sheets of flame, as they rushed with lowered heads upon Jason; but he never flinched a step. The flame of their breath swept round him, but it singed not a hair of his head, and the bulls stopped short and trembled when Medeia began her spell.

Then Jason sprang upon the nearest and seized him by the horn; and up and down they wrestled, till the bull fell grovelling on his knees; for the heart of the brute died within him, and his mighty limbs were loosed, beneath the steadfast eye of that dark witch-maiden and the magic whisper of her lips.

So both the bulls were tamed and yoked;

K

and Jason bound them to the plough, and goaded them onward with his lance till he had ploughed the sacred field.

And all the Minuai shouted; but Aietes bit his lips with rage, for the half of Jason's work was over, and the sun was yet high in heaven.

Then he took the serpents' teeth and sowed them, and waited what would befall. But Medeia looked at him and at his helmet, lest he should forget the lesson she had taught.

And every furrow heaved and bubbled, and out of every clod arose a man. Out of the earth they rose by thousands, each clad from head to foot in steel, and drew their swords and rushed on Jason, where he stood in the midst alone.

Then the Minuai grew pale with fear for him, but Aietes laughed a bitter laugh. "See! if I had not warriors enough already round me, I could call them out of the bosom of the earth."

But Jason snatched off his helmet, and hurled it into the thickest of the throng. And blind madness came upon them, suspicion, hate, and fear; and one cried to his fellow,

" Thou didst strike me! " and another, " Thou art Jason; thou shalt die! " So fury seized those earth-born phantoms, and each turned his hand against the rest; and they fought and were never weary, till they all lay dead upon the ground. Then the magic furrows opened, and the kind earth took them home into her breast; and the grass grew up all green again above them, and Jason's work was done.

Then the Minuai rose and shouted, till Prometheus heard them from his crag. And Jason cried, " Lead me to the fleece this moment, before the sun goes down."

But Aietes thought, " He has conquered the bulls, and sown and reaped the deadly crop. Who is this who is proof against all magic? He may kill the serpent yet." So he delayed, and sat taking counsel with his princes till the sun went down and all was dark. Then he bade a herald cry, " Every man to his home for to-night. To-morrow we will meet these heroes, and speak about the golden fleece."

Then he turned and looked at Medcia. " This is your doing, false witch-maid! You have helped these yellow-haired strangers, and brought shame upon your father and yourself! "

Medeia shrank and trembled, and her face grew pale with fear; and Aietes knew that she was guilty, and whispered, "If they win the fleece, you die!"

But the Minuai marched toward their ship, growling like lions cheated of their prey; for they saw that Aietes meant to mock them, and to cheat them out of all their toil. And Oileus said, "Let us go to the grove together, and take the fleece by force."

And Idas the rash cried, "Let us draw lots who shall go in first; for, while the dragon is devouring one, the rest can slay him and carry off the fleece in peace." But Jason held them back, though he praised them; for he hoped for Medeia's help.

And after awhile Medeia came trembling, and wept a long while before she spoke. And at last—

"My end is come, and I must die; for my father has found out that I have helped you. You he would kill if he dared; but he will not harm you, because you have been his guests. Go then, go, and remember poor Medeia when you are far away across the sea."

But all the heroes cried—

"If you die, we die with you; for without you we cannot win the fleece, and home we will not go without it, but fall here fighting to the last man."

"You need not die," said Jason. "Flee home with us across the sea. Show us first how to win the fleece; for you can do it. Why else are you the priestess of the grove? Show us but how to win the fleece, and come with us, and you shall be my queen, and rule over the rich princes of the Minuai, in Iolcos by the sea."

And all the heroes pressed round, and vowed to her that she should be their queen.

Medeia wept, and shuddered, and hid her face in her hands; for her heart yearned after her sisters and her playfellows, and the home where she was brought up as a child. But at last she looked up at Jason, and spoke between her sobs—

"Must I leave my home and my people, to wander with strangers across the sea? The lot is cast, and I must endure it. I will show you how to win the golden fleece. Bring up your ship to the wood-side, and moor her there against the bank; and let Jason come up at midnight, and one brave comrade with him, and meet me beneath the wall."

Then all the heroes cried together, " I will go!" "and I!" "and I!" And Idas the rash grew mad with envy, for he longed to be foremost in all things. But Medeia calmed them, and said, " Orpheus shall go with Jason, and bring his magic harp, for I hear of him that he is the king of all minstrels, and can charm all things on earth."

And Orpheus laughed for joy, and clapped his hands, because the choice had fallen on him ; for in those days poets and singers were as bold warriors as the best.

So at midnight they went up the bank, and found Medeia ; and beside came Absyrtus her young brother, leading a yearling lamb.

Then Medeia brought them to a thicket beside the War-god's gate; and there she bade Jason dig a ditch, and kill the lamb, and leave it there, and strew on it magic herbs and honey from the honeycomb.

Then sprang up through the earth, with the red fire flashing before her, Brimo the wild witch-huntress, while her mad hounds howled around. She had one head like a horse's, and

another like a ravening hound's, and another
like a hissing snake's, and a sword in either
hand. And she leapt into the ditch with her
hounds, and they ate and drank their fill, while
Jason and Orpheus trembled, and Medeia
hid her eyes. And at last the witch-queen
vanished, and fled with her hounds into the
woods; and the bars of the gates fell down,
and the brazen doors flew wide, and Medeia
and the heroes ran forward and hurried through
the poison wood, among the dark stems of the
mighty beeches, guided by the gleam of the
golden fleece, until they saw it hanging on one
vast tree in the midst. And Jason would have
sprung to seize it; but Medeia held him back,
and pointed, shuddering, to the tree-foot, where
the mighty serpent lay, coiled in and out
among the roots, with a body like a mountain
pine. His coils stretched many a fathom,
spangled with bronze and gold; and half of
him they could see, but no more, for the rest
lay in the darkness far beyond.

And when he saw them coming he lifted up
his head, and watched them with his small
bright eyes, and flashed his forked tongue, and
roared like the fire among the woodlands, till

the forest tossed and groaned. For his cries shook the trees from leaf to root, and swept over the long reaches of the river, and over Aietes' hall, and woke the sleepers in the city, till mothers clasped their children in their fear.

But Medeia called gently to him, and he stretched out his long spotted neck, and licked her hand, and looked up in her face, as if to ask for food. Then she made a sign to Orpheus, and he began his magic song.

And as he sung, the forest grew calm again, and the leaves on every tree hung still; and the serpent's head sank down, and his brazen coils grew limp, and his glittering eyes closed lazily, till he breathed as gently as a child, while Orpheus called to pleasant Slumber, who gives peace to men, and beasts, and waves.

Then Jason leapt forward warily, and stept across that mighty snake, and tore the fleece from off the tree-trunk; and the four rushed down the garden to the bank where the *Argo* lay.

There was a silence for a moment, while Jason held the golden fleece on high. Then he cried, "Go now, good *Argo*, swift and steady, if ever you would see Pelion more."

And she went, as the heroes drove her, grim and silent all, with muffled oars, till the pine-wood bent like willow in their hands, and stout *Argo* groaned beneath their strokes.

On and on, beneath the dewy darkness, they fled swifty down the swirling stream; underneath black walls, and temples, and the castles of the princes of the East; past sluice-mouths, and fragrant gardens, and groves of all strange fruits; past marshes where fat kine lay sleeping, and long beds of whispering reeds; till they heard the merry music of the surge upon the bar, as it tumbled in the moonlight all alone.

Into the surge they rushed, and *Argo* leapt the breakers like a horse, for she knew the time was come to show her mettle, and win honour for the heroes and herself.

Into the surge they rushed, and *Argo* leapt the breakers like a horse, till the heroes stopped all panting, each man upon his oar, as she slid into the still broad sea.

Then Orpheus took his harp and sang a pæan, till the heroes' hearts rose high again; and they rowed on stoutly and steadfastly, away into the darkness of the West.

PART V

SO they fled away in haste to the westward;
but Aietes manned his fleet and followed
them. And Lynceus the quick-eyed saw him
coming, while he was still many a mile away,
and cried, " I see a hundred ships, like a flock
of white swans, far in the east." And at that
they rowed hard, like heroes; but the ships
came nearer every hour.

Then Medeia, the dark-witch-maiden, laid a
cruel and a cunning plot; for she killed Absyrtus her young brother, and cast him into the
sea, and said, " Ere my father can take up his
corpse and bury it, he must wait long, and be
left far behind."

And all the heroes shuddered, and looked
one at the other for shame; yet they did not

punish that dark witch-woman, because she had won for them the golden fleece.

And when Aietes came to the place he saw the floating corpse; and he stopped a long while, and bewailed his son, and took him up, and went home. But he sent on his sailors toward the westward, and bound them by a mighty curse—" Bring back to me that dark witch-woman, that she may die a dreadful death. But if you return without her, you shall die by the same death yourselves."

So the Argonauts escaped for that time: but Father Zeus saw that foul crime; and out of the heavens he sent a storm, and swept the ship far from her course. Day after day the storm drove her, amid foam and blinding mist, till they knew no longer where they were, for the sun was blotted from the skies. And at last the ship struck on a shoal, amid low isles of mud and sand, and the waves rolled over her and through her, and the heroes lost all hope of life.

Then Jason cried to Hera, " Fair queen, who hast befriended us till now, why hast thou left us in our misery, to die here among unknown seas? It is hard to lose the honour which we have won with such toil and danger, and hard never to see Hellas again, and the pleasant bay of Pagasai."

Then out and spoke the magic bough which stood upon the *Argo's* beak, " Because Father Zeus is angry, all this has fallen on you ; for a cruel crime has been done on board, and the sacred ship is foul with blood."

At that some of the heroes cried, "Medeia is the murderess. Let the witch-woman bear her sin, and die!" And they seized Medeia, to hurl her into the sea, and atone for the young boy's death ; but the magic bough spoke again, "Let her live till her crimes are full. Vengeance waits for her, slow and sure ; but she must live, for you need her still. She must show you the way to her sister Circe, who lives among the islands of the West. To her you must sail, a weary way, and she shall cleanse you from your guilt."

Then all the heroes wept aloud when they heard the sentence of the oak ; for they knew that a dark journey lay before them, and years of bitter toil. And some upbraided the dark witch-woman, and some said, " Nay, we are her debtors still ; without her we should never have

won the fleece." But most of them bit their
lips in silence, for they feared the witch's spells.

And now the sea grew calmer, and the sun
shone out once more, and the heroes thrust the
ship off the sand-bank, and rowed forward on
their weary course under the guiding of the
dark witch-maiden, into the wastes of the
unknown sea.

Whither they went I cannot tell, nor how
they came to Circe's isle. Some say that they
went to the westward, and up the Ister * stream,
and so came into the Adriatic, dragging their
ship over the snowy Alps. And others say
that they went southward, into the Red Indian
Sea, and past the sunny lands where spices
grow, round Æthiopia toward the West; and
that at last they came to Libya, and dragged
their ship across the burning sands, and over
the hills into the Syrtes, where the flats and
quicksands spread for many a mile, between
rich Cyrene and the Lotus-eaters' shore. But
all these are but dreams and fables, and dim
hints of unknown lands.

But all say that they came to a place where
they had to drag their ship across the land nine

* The Danube.

days with ropes and rollers, till they came into an unknown sea. And the best of all the old songs tells us how they went away toward the North, till they came to the slope of Caucasus, where it sinks into the sea; and to the narrow Cimmerian Bosphorus,* where the Titan swam across upon the bull; and thence into the lazy waters of the still Mæotid lake.† And thence they went northward ever, up the Tanais, which we call Don, past the Geloni and Sauromatai, and many a wandering shepherd-tribe, and the one-eyed Arimaspi, of whom old Greek poets tell, who steal the gold from the Griffins, in the cold Riphaian hills.‡

And they passed the Scythian archers, and the Tauri who eat men, and the wandering Hyperboreai, who feed their flocks beneath the pole-star, until they came into the northern ocean, the dull dead Cronian Sea.§ And there *Argo* would move on no longer; and each man clasped his elbow, and leaned his head upon his hand, heart-broken with toil and hunger, and gave himself up to death. But brave Ancaios the helmsman cheered up their hearts

* Between the Crimæa and Circassia.   † The Sea of Azov.
‡ The Ural Mountains?   § The Baltic?

once more, and bade them leap on land, and
haul the ship with ropes and rollers for many a
weary day, whether over land, or mud, or ice, I
know not, for the song is mixed and broken
like a dream. And it says next, how they
came to the rich nation of the famous long-
lived men ; and to the coast of the Cimmerians,
who never saw the sun, buried deep in the
glens of the snow mountains; and to the fair
land of Hermione, where dwelt the most
righteous of all nations; and to the gates of
the world below, and to the dwelling-place of
dreams.

And at last Ancaios shouted, " Endure a
little while, brave friends, the worst is surely
past ; for I can see the pure west wind ruffle
the water, and hear the roar of ocean on the
sands. So raise up the mast, and set the sail,
and face what comes like men."

Then out spoke the magic bough, " Ah,
would that I had perished long ago, and been
whelmed by the dread blue rocks, beneath the
fierce swell of the Euxine ! Better so, than
to wander for ever, disgraced by the guilt of
my princes ; for the blood of Absyrtus still
tracks me, and woe follows hard upon woe.

And now some dark horror will clutch me if I come near the Isle of Ierne.* Unless you will cling to the land, and sail southward and southward for ever, I shall wander beyond the Atlantic, to the ocean which has no shore."

Then they blest the magic bough, and sailed southward along the land. But ere they could pass Ierne, the land of mists and storms, the wild wind came down, dark and roaring, and caught the sail, and strained the ropes. And away they drove twelve nights, on the wide wild western sea, through the foam, and over the rollers, while they saw neither sun nor stars. And they cried again, "We shall perish, for we know not where we are. We are lost in the dreary damp darkness, and cannot tell north from south."

But Lynceus the long-sighted called gaily from the bows, "Take heart again, brave sailors; for I see a pine-clad isle, and the halls of the kind Earth-mother, with a crown of clouds around them."

But Orpheus said, "Turn from them, for no living man can land there : there is no harbour on the coast, but steep-walled cliffs all round."

* Britain?

So Ancaios turned the ship away; and for three days more they sailed on, till they came to Aiaia, Circe's home, and the fairy island of the West.*

And there Jason bid them land, and seek about for any sign of living man. And as they went inland Circe met them, coming down toward the ship; and they trembled when they saw her, for her hair, and face, and robes shone like flame.

And she came and looked at Medeia; and Medeia hid her face beneath her veil.

And Circe cried, "Ah, wretched girl, have you forgotten all your sins, that you come hither to my island, where the flowers bloom all the year round? Where is your aged father, and the brother whom you killed? Little do I expect you to return in safety with these strangers whom you love. I will send you food and wine: but your ship must not stay here, for it is foul with sin, and foul with sin its crew."

And the heroes prayed her, but in vain, and cried, "Cleanse us from our guilt!" But she sent them away, and said, "Go on to Malea,

* The Azores?

L

and there you may be cleansed, and return home."

Then a fair wind rose, and they sailed eastward, by Tartessus on the Iberian shore, till they came to the Pillars of Hercules, and the Mediterranean Sea. And thence they sailed on through the deeps of Sardinia, and past the Ausonian islands, and the capes of the Tyrrhenian shore, till they came to a flowery island, upon a still bright summer's eve. And as they neared it, slowly and wearily, they heard sweet songs upon the shore. But when Medeia heard it, she started, and cried, " Beware, all heroes, for these are the rocks of the Sirens. You must pass close by them, for there is no other channel ; but those who listen to that song are lost."

Then Orpheus spoke, the king of all minstrels, " Let them match their song against mine. I have charmed stones, and trees, and dragons, how much more the hearts of men ! " So he caught up his lyre, and stood upon the poop, and began his magic song.

And now they could see the Sirens on Anthemousa, the flowery isle ; three fair maidens sitting on the beach, beneath a red rock in the setting sun, among beds of crimson poppies and golden asphodel. Slowly they sung and sleepily, with silver voices, mild and clear, which stole over the golden waters, and into the hearts of all the heroes, in spite of Orpheus' song.

And all things stayed around and listened; the gulls sat in white lines along the rocks; on the beach great seals lay basking, and kept time with lazy heads; while silver shoals of fish came up to hearken, and whispered as they broke the shining calm. The Wind overhead hushed his whistling, as he shepherded his clouds toward the west; and the clouds stood in mid blue, and listened dreaming, like a flock of golden sheep.

And as the heroes listened, the oars fell from their hands, and their heads drooped on their breasts, and they closed their heavy eyes; and they dreamed of bright still gardens, and of slumbers under murmuring pines, till all their toil seemed foolishness, and they thought of their renown no more.

Then one lifted his head suddenly, and cried, "What use in wandering for ever? Let us stay here and rest awhile." And another,

"Let us row to the shore, and hear the words they sing." And another, "I care not for the words, but for the music. They shall sing me to sleep, that I may rest."

And Butes, the son of Pandion, the fairest of all mortal men, leapt out and swam toward the shore, crying, "I come, I come, fair maidens, to live and die here, listening to your song."

Then Medeia clapped her hands together, and cried, "Sing louder, Orpheus, sing a bolder strain; wake up these hapless sluggards, or none of them will see the land of Hellas more."

Then Orpheus lifted his harp, and crashed his cunning hand across the strings; and his music and his voice rose like a trumpet through the still evening air; into the air it rushed like thunder, till the rocks rang and the sea; and into their souls it rushed like wine, till all hearts beat fast within their breasts.

And he sung the song of Perseus, how the Gods led him over land and sea, and how he slew the loathly Gorgon, and won himself a peerless bride; and how he sits now with the Gods upon Olympus, a shining star in the sky, immortal with his immortal bride, and honoured by all men below.

So Orpheus sang, and the Sirens, answering each other across the golden sea, till Orpheus' voice drowned the Sirens', and the heroes caught their oars again.

And they cried, "We will be men like Perseus, and we will dare and suffer to the last. Sing us his song again, brave Orpheus, that we may forget the Sirens and their spell."

And as Orpheus sang, they dashed their oars into the sea, and kept time to his music, as they fled fast away; and the Sirens' voices died behind them, in the hissing of the foam along their wake.

But Butes swam to the shore, and knelt down before the Sirens, and cried, "Sing on! Sing on!" But he could say no more, for a charmed sleep came over him, and a pleasant humming in his ears; and he sank all along upon the pebbles, and forgot all heaven and earth, and never looked at that sad beach around him, all strewn with the bones of men.

Then slowly rose up those three fair sisters, with a cruel smile upon their lips; and slowly they crept down towards him, like leopards who creep upon their prey; and their hands were like the talons of eagles as they stept across the bones of their victims to enjoy their cruel feast.

But fairest Aphrodite saw him from the highest Idalian peak, and she pitied his youth and his beauty, and leapt up from her golden throne; and like a falling star she cleft the sky, and left a trail of glittering light, till she stooped to the Isle of the Sirens, and snatched their prey from their claws. And she lifted Butes as he lay sleeping, and wrapt him in a golden mist; and she bore him to the peak of Lilybæum, and he slept there many a pleasant year.

But when the Sirens saw that they were conquered, they shrieked for envy and rage, and leapt from the beach into the sea, and were changed into rocks until this day.

Then they came to the straits by Lilybæum, and saw Sicily, the three-cornered island, under which Enceladus the giant lies groaning day and night, and when he turns the earth quakes, and his breath bursts out in roaring flames from the highest cone of Ætna, above the chestnut woods. And there Charybdis caught

them in its fearful coils of wave, and rolled
mast-high about them, and spun them round
and round; and they could go neither back
nor forward, while the whirlpool sucked them
in.

And while they struggled they saw near
them, on the other side the strait, a rock stand
in the water, with its peak wrapt round in
clouds—a rock which no man could climb,
though he had twenty hands and feet, for
the stone was smooth and slippery, as if
polished by man's hand; and half-way up a
misty cave looked out toward the west.

And when Orpheus saw it he groaned, and
struck his hands together. And "Little will it
help us," he cried, "to escape the jaws of the
whirlpool; for in that cave lives Scylla, the
sea-hag with a young whelp's voice; my mother
warned me of her ere we sailed away from
Hellas; she has six heads, and six long necks,
and hides in that dark cleft. And from her
cave she fishes for all things which pass by—
for sharks, and seals, and dolphins, and all the
herds of Amphitrite. And never ship's crew
boasted that they came safe by her rock, for she
bends her long necks down to them, and every

mouth takes up a man. And who will help us now? For Hera and Zeus hate us, and our ship is foul with guilt; so we must die, whatever befalls."

Then out of the depths came Thetis, Peleus' silver-footed bride, for love of her gallant husband, and all her nymphs around her; and they played like snow-white dolphins, diving on from wave to wave, before the ship, and in her wake, and beside her, as dolphins play. And they caught the ship, and guided her, and passed her on from hand to hand, and tossed her through the billows, as maidens toss the ball. And when Scylla stooped to seize her, they struck back her ravening heads, and foul Scylla whined, as a whelp whines, at the touch of their gentle hands. But she shrank into her cave affrighted; for all bad things shrink from good; and *Argo* leapt safe past her, while a fair breeze rose behind. Then Thetis and her nymphs sank down to their coral caves beneath the sea, and their gardens of green and purple, where live flowers bloom all the year round; while the heroes went on rejoicing, yet dreading what might come next.

After that they rowed on steadily for many a

weary day, till they saw a long high island, and
beyond it a mountain land. And they searched
till they found a harbour, and there rowed
boldly in. But after awhile they stopped, and
wondered, for there stood a great city on the
shore, and temples and walls and gardens, and
castles high in air upon the cliffs. And on
either side they saw a harbour, with a narrow
mouth, but wide within; and black ships without number, high and dry upon the shore.

Then Ancaios, the wise helmsman, spoke,
"What new wonder is this? I know all isles,
and harbours, and the windings of all seas;
and this should be Corcyra, where a few wild
goat-herds dwell. But whence come these new
harbours and vast works of polished stone?"

But Jason said, "They can be no savage
people. We will go in and take our chance."

So they rowed into the harbour, among a
thousand black-beaked ships, each larger far
than *Argo*, toward a quay of polished stone.
And they wondered at that mighty city, with
its roofs of burnished brass, and long and lofty
walls of marble, with strong palisades above.
And the quays were full of people, merchants,
and mariners, and slaves, going to and fro with

merchandise among the crowd of ships. And the heroes' hearts were humbled, and they looked at each other and said, "We thought ourselves a gallant crew when we sailed from Iolcos by the sea; but how small we look before this city, like an ant before a hive of bees."

Then the sailors hailed them roughly from the quay, "What men are you?—we want no strangers here, nor pirates. We keep our business to ourselves."

But Jason answered gently, with many a flattering word, and praised their city and their harbour, and their fleet of gallant ships. "Surely you are the children of Poseidon, and the masters of the sea; and we are but poor wandering mariners, worn out with thirst and toil. Give us but food and water, and we will go on our voyage in peace."

Then the sailors laughed, and answered, "Stranger, you are no fool; you talk like an honest man, and you shall find us honest too. We are the children of Poseidon, and the masters of the sea; but come ashore to us, and you shall have the best that we can give."

So they limped ashore, all stiff and weary, with long ragged beards and sunburnt cheeks, and garments torn and weather-stained, and weapons rusted with the spray, while the sailors laughed at them (for they were rough-tongued, though their hearts were frank and kind). And one said, " These fellows are but raw sailors; they look as if they had been sea-sick all the day." And another, " Their legs have grown crooked with much rowing, till they waddle in their walk like ducks."

At that Idas the rash would have struck them; but Jason held him back, till one of the merchant kings spoke to them, a tall and stately man.

" Do not be angry, strangers; the sailor boys must have their jest. But we will treat you justly and kindly, for strangers and poor men come from God; and you seem no common sailors by your strength, and height, and weapons. Come up with me to the palace of Alcinous, the rich sea-going king, and we will feast you well and heartily; and after that you shall tell us your name."

But Medeia hung back, and trembled, and whispered in Jason's ear, " We are betrayed, and are going to our ruin, for I see my country-men among the crowd; dark-eyed Colchi in steel mail-shirts, such as they wear in my father's land."

"It is too late to turn," said Jason. And he spoke to the merchant king, "What country is this, good sir; and what is this new-built town?"

"This is the land of the Phæaces, beloved by all the Immortals; for they come hither and feast like friends with us, and sit by our side in the hall. Hither we came from Liburnia to escape the unrighteous Cyclopes; for they robbed us, peaceful merchants, of our hard-earned wares and wealth. So Nausithous, the son of Poseidon, brought us hither, and died in peace; and now his son Alcinous rules us, and Arete the wisest of queens."

So they went up across the square, and wondered still more as they went; for along the quays lay in order great cables, and yards, and masts, before the fair temple of Poseidon, the blue-haired king of the seas. And round the square worked the shipwrights, as many in number as ants, twining ropes, and hewing timber, and smoothing long yards and oars.

And the Minuai went on in silence through clean white marble streets, till they came to the hall of Alcinous, and they wondered then still more. For the lofty palace shone aloft in the sun, with walls of plated brass, from the threshold to the innermost chamber, and the doors were of silver and gold. And on each side of the doorway sat living dogs of gold, who never grew old or died, so well Hephaistos had made them in his forges in smoking Lemnos, and gave them to Alcinous to guard his gates by night. And within, against the walls, stood thrones on either side, down the whole length of the hall, strewn with rich glossy shawls ; and on them the merchant kings of those crafty sea-roving Phæaces sat eating and drinking in pride, and feasting there all the year round. And boys of molten gold stood each on a polished altar, and held torches in their hands, to give light all night to the guests. And round the house sat fifty maid-servants, some grinding the meal in the mill, some turning the spindle, some weaving at the loom, while their hands twinkled as they passed the shuttle, like quivering aspen leaves.

And outside before the palace a great garden was walled round, filled full of stately fruit-trees, gray olives and sweet figs, and pomegranates, pears, and apples, which bore the whole year round. For the rich south-west wind fed them, till pear grew ripe on pear, fig on fig, and grape on grape, all the winter and the spring. And at the farther end gay flower-beds bloomed through all seasons of the year; and two fair fountains rose, and ran, one through the garden grounds, and one beneath the palace gate, to water all the town. Such noble gifts the heavens had given to Alcinous the wise.

So they went in, and saw him sitting, like Poseidon, on his throne, with his golden sceptre by him, in garments stiff with gold, and in his hand a sculptured goblet, as he pledged the merchant kings; and beside him stood Arete, his wise and lovely queen, and leaned against a pillar as she spun her golden threads.

Then Alcinous rose, and welcomed them, and bade them sit and eat; and the servants brought them tables, and bread, and meat, and wine.

But Medeia went on trembling toward Arete the fair queen, and fell at her knees, and clasped them, and cried, weeping, as she knelt—

" I am your guest, fair queen, and I entreat you by Zeus, from whom prayers come. Do not send me back to my father to die some dreadful death; but let me go my way, and bear my burden. Have I not had enough of punishment and shame ? "

" Who are you, strange maiden ? and what is the meaning of your prayer ? "

" I am Medeia, daughter of Aietes, and I saw my countrymen here to-day; and I know that they are come to find me, and take me home to die some dreadful death."

Then Arete frowned and said, " Lead this girl in, my maidens; and let the kings decide, not I."

And Alcinous leapt up from his throne, and cried, " Speak, strangers, who are you? And who is this maiden ? "

" We are the heroes of the Minuai," said Jason; " and this maiden has spoken truth. We are the men who took the golden fleece, the men whose fame has run round every shore. We came hither out of the ocean, after sorrows such as man never saw before. We went out many, and come back few, for many a noble comrade have we lost. So let us go, as you should let your guests go, in peace; that the world may say, 'Alcinous is a just king.'"

But Alcinous frowned, and stood deep in thought, and at last he spoke—

"Had not the deed been done which is done, I should have said this day to myself, 'It is an honour to Alcinous, and to his children after him, that the far-famed Argonauts are his guests.' But these Colchi are my guests, as you are, and for this month they have waited here with all their fleet, for they have hunted all the seas of Hellas, and could not find you, and dared neither go farther, nor go home."

"Let them choose out their champions, and we will fight them, man for man."

"No guests of ours shall fight upon our island, and if you go outside they will outnumber you. I will do justice between you, for I know and do what is right."

Then he turned to his kings and said, "This

may stand over till to-morrow. To-night we will feast our guests, and hear the story of all their wanderings, and how they came hither out of the ocean."

So Alcinous bade the servants take the heroes in, and bathe them, and give them clothes. And they were glad when they saw the warm water, for it was long since they had bathed. And they washed off the sea-salt from their limbs, and anointed themselves from head to foot with oil, and combed out their golden hair. Then they came back again into the hall, while the merchant kings rose up to do them honour. And each man said to his neighbour, " No wonder that these men won fame. How they stand now like Giants, or Titans, or Immortals come down from Olympus, though many a winter has worn them, and many a fearful storm. What must they have been when they sailed from Iolcos, in the bloom of their youth, long ago?"

Then they went out to the garden ; and the merchant princes said, " Heroes, run races with us. Let us see whose feet are nimblest."

" We cannot race against you, for our limbs are stiff from sea; and we have lost our two

M

swift comrades, the sons of the north wind.
But do not think us cowards: if you wish to
try our strength, we will shoot, and box, and
wrestle, against any men on earth."

And Alcinous smiled, and answered, "I
believe you, gallant guests; with your long
limbs and broad shoulders, we could never
match you here. For we care nothing here
for boxing, or for shooting with the bow; but
for feasts, and songs, and harping, and dancing,
and running races, to stretch our limbs on
shore."

So they danced there and ran races, the jolly
merchant kings, till the night fell, and all went
in.

And then they ate and drank, and comforted
their weary souls, till Alcinous called a herald,
and bade him go and fetch the harper.

The herald went out, and fetched the harper,
and led him in by the hand; and Alcinous cut
him a piece of meat, from the fattest of the
haunch, and sent it to him, and said, "Sing
to us, noble harper, and rejoice the heroes'
hearts."

So the harper played and sang, while the
dancers danced strange figures; and after that

the tumblers showed their tricks, till the heroes laughed again.

Then, " Tell me, heroes," asked Alcinous, "you who have sailed the ocean round, and seen the manners of all nations, have you seen such dancers as ours here, or heard such music and such singing ? We hold ours to be the best on earth."

" Such dancing we have never seen," said Orpheus ; "and your singer is a happy man, for Phœbus himself must have taught him, or else he is the son of a Muse, as I am also, and have sung once or twice, though not so well as he."

" Sing to us, then, noble stranger," said Alcinous ; "and we will give you precious gifts."

So Orpheus took his magic harp, and sang to them a stirring song of their voyage from Iolcos, and their dangers, and how they won the golden fleece ; and of Medeia's love, and how she helped them, and went with them over land and sea ; and of all their fearful dangers, from monsters, and rocks, and storms, till the heart of Arete was softened, and all the women wept. And the merchant kings rose up, each man from off his golden throne, and clapped their hands, and shouted, " Hail to the noble Argonauts, who sailed the unknown sea ! "

Then he went on, and told their journey over the sluggish northern main, and through the shoreless outer ocean, to the fairy island of the west ; and of the Sirens, and Scylla, and Charybdis, and all the wonders they had seen, till midnight passed and the day dawned ; but the kings never thought of sleep. Each man sat still and listened, with his chin upon his hand.

And at last, when Orpheus had ended, they all went thoughtful out, and the heroes lay down to sleep, beneath the sounding porch outside, where Arete had strewn them rugs and carpets, in the sweet still summer night.

But Arete pleaded hard with her husband for Medeia, for her heart was softened. And she said, " The Gods will punish her, not we. After all, she is our guest and my suppliant, and prayers are the daughters of Zeus. And who, too, dare part man and wife, after all they have endured together ? "

And Alcinous smiled. " The minstrel's song

has charmed you : but I must remember what is right, for songs cannot alter justice; and I must be faithful to my name. Alcinous I am called, the man of sturdy sense ; and Alcinous I will be." But for all that Arete besought him, until she won him round.

So next morning he sent a herald, and called the kings into the square, and said, " This is a puzzling matter : remember but one thing. These Minuai live close by us, and we may meet them often on the seas ; but Aietes lives afar off, and we have only heard his name. Which, then, of the two is it safer to offend— the men near us, or the men far off ? "

The princes laughed, and praised his wisdom ; and Alcinous called the heroes to the square, and the Colchi also; and they came and stood opposite each other, but Medeia stayed in the palace. Then Alcinous spoke, " Heroes of the Colchi, what is your errand about this lady ? "

" To carry her home with us, that she may die a shameful death ; but if we return without her, we must die the death she should have died."

" What say you to this, Jason the Æolid ? " said Alcinous, turning to the Minuai.

"I say," said the cunning Jason, "that they are come here on a bootless errand. Do you think that you can make her follow you, heroes of the Colchi—her, who knows all spells and charms? She will cast away your ships on quicksands, or call down on you Brimo the wild huntress; or the chains will fall from off her wrists, and she will escape in her dragon-car; or if not thus, some other way, for she has a thousand plans and wiles. And why return home at all, brave heroes, and face the long seas again, and the Bosphorus, and the stormy Euxine, and double all your toil? There is many a fair land round these coasts, which waits for gallant men like you. Better to settle there, and build a city, and let Aietes and Colchis help themselves."

Then a murmur rose among the Colchi, and some cried, "He has spoken well"; and some, "We have had enough of roving, we will sail the seas no more!" And the chief said at last, "Be it so, then; a plague she has been to us, and a plague to the house of her father, and a plague she will be to you. Take her, since you are no wiser; and we will sail away toward the north."

Then Alcinous gave them food and water, and garments, and rich presents of all sorts; and he gave the same to the Minuai, and sent them all away in peace.

So Jason kept the dark witch-maiden to breed him woe and shame; and the Colchi went northward into the Adriatic, and settled, and built towns along the shore.

Then the heroes rowed away to the eastward, to reach Hellas, their beloved land; but a storm came down upon them, and swept them far away toward the south. And they rowed till they were spent with struggling, through the darkness and the blinding rain; but where they were they could not tell, and they gave up all hope of life. And at last they touched the ground, and when daylight came they waded to the shore; and saw nothing round but sand and desolate salt pools, for they had come to the quicksands of the Syrtis, and the dreary treeless flats which lie between Numidia and Cyrene, on the burning shore of Africa. And there they wandered starving for many a weary day, ere they could launch their ship again, and gain the open sea. And there Canthus was killed, while he was trying to drive off sheep, by a stone which a herdsman threw.

And there too Mopsus died, the seer who knew the voices of all birds; but he could not foretell his own end, for he was bitten in the foot by a snake, one of those which sprang from the Gorgon's head when Perseus carried it across the sands.

At last they rowed away toward the northward, for many a weary day, till their water was spent, and their food eaten; and they were worn out with hunger and thirst. But at last they saw a long steep island, and a blue peak high among the clouds; and they knew it for the peak of Ida, and the famous land of Crete. And they said, "We will land in Crete, and see Minos the just king, and all his glory and his wealth; at least he will treat us hospitably, and let us fill our water-casks upon the shore."

But when they came nearer to the island they saw a wondrous sight upon the cliffs. For on a cape to the westward stood a giant, taller than any mountain pine, who glittered aloft against the sky like a tower of burnished brass. He turned and looked on all sides

round him, till he saw the *Argo* and her crew;
and when he saw them he came toward them,
more swiftly than the swiftest horse, leaping
across the glens at a bound, and striding at
one step from down to down. And when he
came abreast of them he brandished his arms
up and down, as a ship hoists and lowers her
yards, and shouted with his brazen throat like
a trumpet from off the hills, "You are pirates,
you are robbers! If you dare land here, you
die."

Then the heroes cried, "We are no pirates.
We are all good men and true, and all we ask
is food and water;" but the giant cried the
more—

"You are robbers, you are pirates all; I
know you; and if you land, you shall die the
death."

Then he waved his arms again as a signal,
and they saw the people flying inland, driving
their flocks before them, while a great flame
arose among the hills. Then the giant ran up
a valley and vanished, and the heroes lay on
their oars in fear.

But Medeia stood watching all from under
her steep black brows, with a cunning smile

upon her lips, and a cunning plot within her heart. At last she spoke, " I know this giant. I heard of him in the East. Hephaistos the Fire King made him in his forge in Ætna beneath the earth, and called him Talus, and gave him to Minos for a servant, to guard the coast of Crete. Thrice a day he walks round the island, and never stops to sleep; and if strangers land he leaps into his furnace, which flames there among the hills; and when he is red-hot he rushes on them, and burns them in his brazen hands."

Then all the heroes cried, " What shall we do, wise Medeia? We must have water, or we die of thirst. Flesh and blood we can face fairly; but who can face this red-hot brass?"

" I can face red-hot brass, if the tale I hear be true. For they say that he has but one vein in all his body, filled with liquid fire; and that this vein is closed with a nail : but I know not where that nail is placed. But if I can get it once into these hands, you shall water your ship here in peace."

Then she bade them put her on shore, and row off again, and wait what would befall.

And the heroes obeyed her unwillingly, for

they were ashamed to leave her so alone; but Jason said, "She is dearer to me than to any of you, yet I will trust her freely on shore; she has more plots than we can dream of in the windings of that fair and cunning head."

So they left the witch-maiden on the shore; and she stood there in her beauty all alone, till the giant strode back red-hot from head to heel, while the grass hissed and smoked beneath his tread.

And when he saw the maiden alone, he stopped; and she looked boldly up into his face without moving, and began her magic song :—

"Life is short, though life is sweet; and even men of brass and fire must die. The brass must rust, the fire must cool, for time gnaws all things in their turn. Life is short, though life is sweet: but sweeter to live for ever; sweeter to live ever youthful like the Gods, who have ichor in their veins—ichor which gives life, and youth, and joy, and a bounding heart."

Then Talus said, "Who are you, strange maiden, and where is this ichor of youth?"

Then Medeia held up a flask of crystal, and

said, "Here is the ichor of youth. I am
Medeia the enchantress; my sister Circe gave
me this, and said, "Go and reward Talus, the
faithful servant, for his fame is gone out into all
lands." So come, and I will pour this into
your veins, that you may live for ever young."

And he listened to her false words, that
simple Talus, and came near; and Medeia
said, "Dip yourself in the sea first, and cool
yourself, lest you burn my tender hands; then
show me where the nail in your vein is, that I
may pour the ichor in."

Then that simple Talus dipped himself in
the sea, till it hissed, and roared, and smoked;
and came and knelt before Medeia, and showed
her the secret nail.

And she drew the nail out gently, but she
poured no ichor in; and instead the liquid fire
spouted forth, like a stream of red-hot iron.
And Talus tried to leap up, crying, "You have
betrayed me, false witch-maiden!" But she
lifted up her hands before him, and sang, till he
sank beneath her spell. And as he sank, his
brazen limbs clanked heavily, and the earth
groaned beneath his weight; and the liquid
fire ran from his heel, like a stream of lava, to

the sea; and Medeia laughed, and called to the heroes, "Come ashore, and water your ship in peace."

So they came, and found the giant lying dead; and they fell down, and kissed Medeia's feet; and watered their ship, and took sheep and oxen, and so left that inhospitable shore.

At last, after many more adventures, they came to the Cape of Malea, at the south-west point of the Peloponnese. And there they offered sacrifices, and Orpheus purged them from their guilt. Then they rode away again to the northward, past the Laconian shore, and came all worn and tired by Sunium, and up the long Eubœan Strait, until they saw once more Pelion, and Aphetai, and Iolcos by the sea.

And they ran the ship ashore; but they had no strength left to haul her up the beach: and they crawled out on the pebbles, and sat down, and wept till they could weep no more. For the houses and the trees were all altered; and all the faces which they saw were strange; and their joy was swallowed up in sorrow, while they thought of their youth, and all their labour, and the gallant comrades they had lost.

And the people crowded round, and asked them, "Who are you, that you sit weeping here?"

"We are the sons of your princes, who sailed out many a year ago. We went to fetch the golden fleece, and we have brought it, and grief therewith. Give us news of our fathers and our mothers, if any of them be left alive on earth."

Then there was shouting, and laughing, and weeping; and all the kings came to the shore, and they led away the heroes to their homes, and bewailed the valiant dead.

Then Jason went up with Medeia to the palace of his uncle Pelias. And when he came in Pelias sat by the hearth, crippled and blind with age; while opposite him sat Æson, Jason's father, crippled and blind likewise; and the two old men's heads shook together as they tried to warm themselves before the fire.

And Jason fell down at his father's knees, and wept, and called him by his name. And the old man stretched his hands out, and felt him, and said, "Do not mock me, young hero. My son Jason is dead long ago at sea."

"I am your own son Jason, whom you

trusted to the Centaur upon Pelion; and I have brought home the golden fleece, and a princess of the Sun's race for my bride. So now give me up the kingdom, Pelias my uncle, and fulfil your promise as I have fulfilled mine."

Then his father clung to him like a child, and wept, and would not let him go; and cried, "Now I shall not go down lonely to my grave. Promise me never to leave me till I die."

PART VI

AND now I wish that I could end my story pleasantly; but it is no fault of mine that I cannot. The old songs end it sadly, and I believe that they are right and wise; for though the heroes were purified at Malea, yet sacrifices cannot make bad hearts good, and Jason had taken a wicked wife, and he had to bear his burden to the last.

And first she laid a cunning plot to punish that poor old Pelias, instead of letting him die in peace.

For she told his daughters, " I can make old things young again ; I will show you how easy it is to do." So she took an old ram and killed him, and put him in a cauldron with magic herbs ; and whispered her spells over him, and he leapt out again a young lamb. So that " Medeia's cauldron " is a proverb still, by which we mean times of war and change, when the world has become old and feeble, and grows young again through bitter pains.

Then she said to Pelias' daughters, " Do to your father as I did to this ram, and he will grow young and strong again." But she only told them half the spell ; so they failed, while Medeia mocked them ; and poor old Pelias died, and his daughters came to misery. But the songs say she cured Æson, Jason's father, and he became young and strong again.

But Jason could not love her, after all her cruel deeds. So he was ungrateful to her, and wronged her ; and she revenged herself on him. And a terrible revenge she took—too terrible to speak of here. But you will hear of it yourselves when you grow up, for it has been sung in noble poetry and music ; and whether it be true or not, it stands for ever as a warning to us not to seek for help from evil persons, or to gain good ends by evil means. For if we use an adder even against our enemies, it will turn again and sting us.

But of all the other heroes there is many a brave tale left, which I have no space to tell you, so you must read them for yourselves ;—

N

of the hunting of the boar in Calydon, which
Meleager killed; and of Heracles' twelve
famous labours; and of the seven who fought
at Thebes; and of the noble love of Castor and
Polydeuces, the twin Dioscouroi—how when
one died the other would not live without him,
so they shared their immortality between them;
and Zeus changed them into the two twin stars
which never rise both at once.

And what became of Cheiron, the good
immortal beast? That, too, is a sad story; for
the heroes never saw him more. He was
wounded by a poisoned arrow, at Pholoe
among the hills, when Heracles opened the
fatal wine-jar, which Cheiron had warned him
not to touch. And the Centaurs smelt the
wine, and flocked to it, and fought for it with
Heracles; but he killed them all with his
poisoned arrows, and Cheiron was left alone.
Then Cheiron took up one of the arrows, and
dropped it by chance upon his foot; and the
poison ran like fire along his veins, and he lay
down and longed to die; and cried, "Through
wine I perish, the bane of all my race. Why
should I live for ever in this agony? Who
will take my immortality, that I may die?

Then Prometheus answered, the good Titan, whom Heracles had set free from Caucasus, "I will take your immortality and live for ever, that I may help poor mortal men." So Cheiron gave him his immortality, and died, and had rest from pain. And Heracles and Prometheus wept over him, and went to bury him on Pelion; but Zeus took him up among the stars, to live for ever, grand and mild, low down in the far southern sky.

And in time the heroes died, all but Nestor, the silver-tongued old man; and left behind them valiant sons, but not so great as they had been. Yet their fame, too, lives till this day, for they fought at the ten years' siege of Troy: and their story is in the book which we call Homer, in two of the noblest songs on earth— the "Iliad," which tells us of the siege of Troy, and Achilles' quarrel with the kings; and the "Odyssey," which tells the wanderings of Odysseus, through many lands for many years, and how Alcinous sent him home at last, safe to Ithaca his beloved island, and to Penelope his faithful wife, and Telemachus his son, and Euphorbus the noble swineherd, and the old dog who licked his hand and died. We will read that sweet story, children, by the fire some winter night.   And now I will end my tale, and begin another and a more cheerful one, of a hero who became a worthy king, and won his people's love.

Story III.—Theseus

PART I

ONCE upon a time there was a princess in Trœzene, Aithra, the daughter of Pittheus the king. She had one fair son, named Theseus, the bravest lad in all the land; and Aithra never smiled but when she looked at him, for her husband had forgotten her, and lived far away. And she used to go up to the mountain above Trœzene, to the temple of Poseidon, and sit there all day looking out across the bay, over Methana, to the purple peaks of Ægina and the Attic shore beyond. And when Theseus was full fifteen years old she took him up with her to the temple, and into the thickets of the grove which grew in the temple-yard. And she led him to a tall plane-tree, beneath whose shade

grew arbutus, and lentisk, and purple heather-
bushes.   And there she sighed, and said,
" Theseus, my son, go into that thicket, and you
will find at the plane-tree foot a great flat stone;
lift it, and bring me what lies underneath."

Then Theseus pushed his way in through
the thick bushes, and saw that they had not
been moved for many a year.   And searching
among their roots he found a great flat stone,
all overgrown with ivy, and acanthus, and moss.
He tried to lift it, but he could not.   And he
tried till the sweat ran down his brow from
heat, and the tears from his eyes for shame;
but all was of no avail.   And at last he came
back to his mother, and said, " I have found
the stone, but I cannot lift it; nor do I think
that any man could in all Trœzene."

Then she sighed, and said, " The Gods wait
long ; but they are just at last.   Let it be for
another year.   The day may come when you
will be a stronger man than lives in all
Trœzene."

Then she took him by the hand, and went
into the temple and prayed, and came down
again with Theseus to her home.

And when a full year was past she led

Theseus up again to the temple and bade him lift the stone, but he could not.

Then she sighed, and said the same words again, and went down, and came again the next year; but Theseus could not lift the stone then, nor the year after; and he longed to ask his mother the meaning of that stone, and what might lie underneath it; but her face was so sad that he had not the heart to ask.

So he said to himself, "The day shall surely come when I will lift that stone, though no man in Trœzene can." And in order to grow strong he spent all his days in wrestling, and boxing, and hurling, and taming horses, and hunting the boar and the bull, and coursing goats and deer among the rocks; till upon all the mountains there was no hunter so swift as Theseus; and he killed Phaia the wild sow of Crommyon, which wasted all the land; till all the people said, "Surely the Gods are with the lad."

And when his eighteenth year was past, Aithra led him up again to the temple, and said, "Theseus, lift the stone this day, or never know who you are." And Theseus went into the thicket, and stood over the stone, and tugged at it; and it moved. Then his spirit swelled within him, and he said, "If I break my heart in my body, it shall up." And he tugged at it once more, and lifted it, and rolled it over with a shout.

And when he looked beneath it, on the ground lay a sword of bronze, with a hilt of glittering gold, and by it a pair of golden sandals; and he caught them up, and burst through the bushes like a wild boar, and leapt to his mother, holding them high above his head.

But when she saw them she wept long in silence, hiding her fair face in her shawl; and Theseus stood by her wondering, and wept also, he knew not why. And when she was tired of weeping she lifted up her head, and laid her finger on her lips, and said, "Hide them in your bosom, Theseus, my son, and come with me where we can look down upon the sea."

Then they went outside the sacred wall, and looked down over the bright blue sea; and Aithra said—

"Do you see this land at our feet?"

And he said, "Yes; this is Trœzene, where I was born and bred."

And she said, "It is but a little land, barren

and rocky, and looks towards the bleak north-east. Do you see that land beyond?"

"Yes; that is Attica, where the Athenian people dwell."

"That is a fair land and large, Theseus my son; and it looks toward the sunny south; a land of olive-oil and honey, the joy of Gods and men. For the Gods have girdled it with mountains, whose veins are of pure silver, and their bones of marble white as snow; and there the hills are sweet with thyme and basil, and the meadows with violet and asphodel, and the nightingales sing all day in the thickets, by the side of ever-flowing streams. There are twelve towns well peopled, the homes of an ancient race, the children of Kekrops the serpent-king, the son of Mother Earth, who wear gold cicalas among the tresses of their golden hair; for like the cicalas they sprang from the earth, and like the cicalas they sing all day, rejoicing in the genial sun. What would you do, son Theseus, if you were king of such a land?"

Then Theseus stood astonished, as he looked across the broad bright sea, and saw the fair Attic shore, from Sunium to Hymettus and Pentelicus, and all the mountain peaks which girdle Athens round. But Athens itself he could not see, for purple Ægina stood before it, midway across the sea.

Then his heart grew great within him, and he said, " If I were king of such a land I would rule it wisely and well in wisdom and in might, that when I died all men might weep over my tomb, and cry, ' Alas for the shepherd of his people ! ' "

And Althra smiled, and said, " Take, then, the sword and the sandals, and go to Ægeus, king of Athens, who lives on Pallas' hill ; and say to him, ' The stone is lifted, but whose is the pledge beneath it ? ' Then show him the sword and the sandals, and take what the Gods shall send."

But Theseus wept, " Shall I leave you, O my mother ? "

But she answered, " Weep not for me. That which is fated must be ; and grief is easy to those who do nought but grieve. Full of sorrow was my youth, and full of sorrow my woman-hood. Full of sorrow was my youth for Bellero-phon, the slayer of the Chimæra, whom my father drove away by treason ; and full of sorrow my womanhood, for thy treacherous father and for thee; and full of sorrow my old age will be (for I see my fate in dreams), when the sons of the Swan shall carry me captive to the hollow vale of Eurotas, till I sail across the seas a slave, the handmaid of the pest of Greece. Yet shall I be avenged, when the golden-haired heroes sail against Troy, and sack the palaces of Ilium; then my son shall set me free from thraldom, and I shall hear the tale of Theseus' fame. Yet beyond that I see new sorrows; but I can bear them as I have borne the past."

Then she kissed Theseus, and wept over him; and went into the temple, and Theseus saw her no more.

PART II

HOW THESEUS SLEW THE DEVOURERS OF MEN

SO Theseus stood there alone, with his mind full of many hopes. And first he thought of going down to the harbour and hiring a swift ship, and sailing across the bay to Athens; but even that seemed too slow for him, and he longed for wings to fly across the sea and find his father. But after a while his heart began to fail him; and he sighed, and said within himself—

"What if my father have other sons about him whom he loves? What if he will not receive me? And what have I done that he should receive me? He has forgotten me ever since I was born: why should he welcome me now?"

Then he thought a long while sadly; and at the last he cried aloud, "Yes! I will make him love me; for I will prove myself worthy of

204

his love. I will win honour and renown, and do such deeds that Ægeus shall be proud of me, though he had fifty other sons! Did not Heracles win himself honour though he was opprest, and the slave of Eurystheus? Did he not kill all robbers and evil beasts, and drain great lakes and marshes, breaking the hills through with his club? Therefore it was that all men honoured him, because he rid them of their miseries, and made life pleasant to them and their children after them. Where can I go, to do as Heracles has done? Where can I find strange adventures, robbers, and monsters, and the children of hell, the enemies of men? I will go by land, and into the mountains, and round by the way of the Isthmus. Perhaps there I may hear of brave adventures, and do something which shall win my father's love."

So he went by land, and away into the mountains, with his father's sword upon his thigh, till he came to the Spider mountains, which hang over Epidaurus and the sea, where the glens run downward from one peak in the midst, as the rays spread in the spider's web.

And he went up into the gloomy glens between the furrowed marble walls till the lowland grew blue beneath his feet and the clouds drove damp about his head.

But he went up and up for ever, through the spider's web of glens, till he could see the narrow gulfs spread below him, north and south, and east and west; black cracks half-choked with mists, and above all a dreary down.

But over that down he must go, for there was no road right or left; so he toiled on through bog and brake, till he came to a pile of stones.

And on the stones a man was sitting, wrapt in a bearskin cloak. The head of the bear served him for a cap, and its teeth grinned white around his brows; and the feet were tied about his throat, and their claws shone white upon his chest. And when he saw Theseus he rose, and laughed till the glens rattled.

"And who art thou, fair fly, who hast walked into the spider's web?" But Theseus walked on steadily, and made no answer; but he thought, "Is this some robber? and has an adventure come already to me?" But the strange man laughed louder than ever, and said—

"Bold fly, know you not that these glens are

the web from which no fly ever finds his way
out again, and this down the spider's house, and
I the spider who sucks the flies? Come hither,
and let me feast upon you; for it is of no use
to run away, so cunning a web has my father
Hephaistos spread for me when he made these
clefts in the mountains, through which no man
finds his way home."

But Theseus came on steadily, and asked—

"And what is your name among men, bold
spider? and where are your spider's fangs?"

Then the strange man laughed again—

"My name is Periphetes, the son of Hephaistos and Anticleia the mountain nymph.
But men call me Corynetes the club-bearer;
and here is my spider's fang."

And he lifted from off the stones at his side
a mighty club of bronze.

"This my father gave me, and forged it
himself in the roots of the mountain; and with
it I pound all proud flies till they give out
their fatness and their sweetness. So give me
up that gay sword of yours, and your mantle,
and your golden sandals, lest I pound you, and
by ill-luck you die."

But Theseus wrapt his mantle round his left

arm quickly, in hard folds, from his shoulder to his hand, and drew his sword, and rushed upon the club-bearer, and the club-bearer rushed on him.

Thrice he struck at Theseus, and made him bend under the blows like a sapling; but Theseus guarded his head with his left arm, and the mantle which was wrapt around it

And thrice Theseus sprang upright after the blow, like a sapling when the storm is past; and he stabbed at the club-bearer with his sword, but the loose folds of the bearskin saved him.

Then Theseus grew mad, and closed with him, and caught him by the throat, and they fell and rolled over together; but when Theseus rose up from the ground the club-bearer lay still at his feet.

Then Theseus took his club and his bear-skin, and left him to the kites and crows, and went upon his journey down the glens on the farther slope, till he came to a broad green valley, and saw flocks and herds sleeping beneath the trees.

And by the side of a pleasant fountain, under the shade of rocks and trees, were nymphs and shepherds dancing; but no one piped to them while they danced.

And when they saw Theseus they shrieked; and the shepherds ran off, and drove away their flocks, while the nymphs dived into the fountain like coots, and vanished.

Theseus wondered and laughed: "What strange fancies have folks here who run away from strangers, and have no music when they dance!" But he was tired, and dusty, and thirsty; so he thought no more of them, but drank and bathed in the clear pool, and then lay down in the shade under a plane-tree, while the water sang him to sleep, as it tinkled down from stone to stone.

And when he woke he heard a whispering, and saw the nymphs peeping at him across the fountain from the dark mouth of a cave, where they sat on green cushions of moss. And one said, "Surely he is not Periphetes;" and another, "He looks like no robber, but a fair and gentle youth."

Then Theseus smiled, and called them, "Fair nymphs, I am not Periphetes. He sleeps among the kites and crows; but I have brought away his bearskin and his club."

Then they leapt across the pool, and came to him, and called the shepherds back. And he told them how he had slain the club-bearer: and the shepherds kissed his feet and sang, " Now we shall feed our flocks in peace, and not be afraid to have music when we dance; for the cruel club-bearer has met his match, and he will listen for our pipes no more."

Then they brought him kid's flesh and wine, and the nymphs brought him honey from the rocks, and he ate, and drank, and slept again, while the nymphs and shepherds danced and sang. And when he woke, they begged him to stay; but he would not. "I have a great work to do," he said; "I must be away toward the Isthmus, that I may go to Athens."

But the shepherds said, "Will you go alone toward Athens? None travel that way now, except in armed troops."

" As for arms, I have enough, as you see. And as for troops, an honest man is good enough company for himself. Why should I not go alone toward Athens?"

" If you do, you must look warily about you on the Isthmus, lest you meet Sinis the robber, whom men call Pituocamptes the pine-bender;

for he bends down two pine-trees, and binds all travellers hand and foot between them, and when he lets the trees go again their bodies are torn in sunder."

"And after that," said another, "you must go inland, and not dare to pass over the cliffs of Sciron; for on the left hand are the mountains, and on the right the sea, so that you have no escape, but must needs meet Sciron the robber, who will make you wash his feet; and while you are washing them he will kick you over the cliff, to the tortoise who lives below, and feeds upon the bodies of the dead."

And before Theseus could answer, another cried, "And after that is a worse danger still, unless you go inland always, and leave Eleusis far on your right. For in Eleusis rules Kerkuon the cruel king, the terror of all mortals, who killed his own daughter Alope in prison. But she was changed into a fair fountain; and her child he cast out upon the mountains, but the wild mares gave it milk. And now he challenges all comers to wrestle with him, for he is the best wrestler in all Attica, and overthrows all who come; and those whom he overthrows he murders miserably, and his palace-court is full of their bones."

Then Theseus frowned, and said, "This seems indeed an ill-ruled land, and adventures enough in it to be tried. But if I am the heir of it, I will rule it and right it, and here is my royal sceptre." And he shook his club of bronze, while the nymphs and shepherds clung round him, and entreated him not to go.

But on he went nevertheless, till he could see both the seas and the citadel of Corinth towering high above all the land. And he past swiftly along the Isthmus, for his heart burned to meet that cruel Sinis; and in a pine-wood at last he met him, where the Isthmus was narrowest and the road ran between high rocks. There he sat upon a stone by the way-side, with a young fir-tree for a club across his knees, and a cord laid ready by his side; and over his head, upon the fir-tops, hung the bones of murdered men.

Then Theseus shouted to him, "Holla, thou valiant pine-bender, hast thou two fir-trees left for me?"

And Sinis leapt to his feet, and answered, pointing to the bones above his head, "My larder has grown empty lately, so I have two fir-trees ready for thee." And he rushed on Theseus, lifting his club, and Theseus rushed upon him.

Then they hammered together till the greenwoods rang; but the metal was tougher than the pine, and Sinis' club broke right across, as the bronze came down upon it. Then Theseus heaved up another mighty stroke, and smote Sinis down upon his face; and knelt upon his back, and bound him with his own cord, and said, " As thou hast done to others, so shall it be done to thee." Then he bent down two young fir-trees, and bound Sinis between them, for all his struggling and his prayers; and let them go, and ended Sinis, and went on, leaving him to the hawks and crows.

Then he went over the hills toward Megara, keeping close along the Saronic Sea, till he came to the cliffs of Sciron, and the narrow path between the mountain and the sea.

And there he saw Sciron sitting by a fountain, at the edge of the cliff. On his knees was a mighty club; and he had barred the path with stones, so that every one must stop who came up.

Then Theseus shouted to him, and said, "Holla, thou tortoise-feeder, do thy feet need washing to-day?"

And Sciron leapt to his feet, and answered—

"My tortoise is empty and hungry, and my feet need washing to-day." And he stood before his barrier, and lifted up his club in both hands.

Then Theseus rushed upon him; and sore was the battle upon the cliff, for when Sciron felt the weight of the bronze club, he dropt his own, and closed with Theseus, and tried to hurl him by main force over the cliff. But Theseus was a wary wrestler, and dropt his own club, and caught him by the throat and by the knee, and forced him back against the wall of stones, and crushed him up against them, till his breath was almost gone. And Sciron cried panting, "Loose me, and I will let thee pass." But Theseus answered, "I must not pass till I have made the rough way smooth;" and he forced him back against the wall till it fell, and Sciron rolled head over heels.

Then Theseus lifted him up all bruised, and said, "Come hither and wash my feet." And he drew his sword, and sat down by the well, and said, " Wash my feet, or I cut you piece-meal."

And Sciron washed his feet trembling ; and when it was done, Theseus rose, and cried, " As thou hast done to others, so shall it be done to thee. Go feed thy tortoise thyself ; " and he kicked him over the cliff into the sea.

And whether the tortoise ate him, I know not ; for some say that earth and sea both disdained to take his body, so foul it was with sin. So the sea cast it out upon the shore, and the shore cast it back into the sea, and at last the waves hurled it high into the air in anger ; and it hung there long without a grave, till it was changed into a desolate rock, which stands there in the surge until this day.

This at least is true, which Pausanias tells, that in the royal porch at Athens he saw the figure of Theseus modelled in clay, and by him Sciron the robber falling headlong into the sea.

Then he went a long day's journey, past Megara, into the Attic land, and high before him rose the snow-peaks of Cithæron, all cold above the black pine-woods, where haunt the

Furies, and the raving Bacchæ, and the Nymphs who drive men wild, far aloft upon the dreary mountains, where the storms howl all day long. And on his right hand was the sea always, and Salamis, with its island cliffs, and the sacred strait of the sea-fight, where afterwards the Persians fled before the Greeks. So he went all day until the evening, till he saw the Thriasian plain, and the sacred city of Eleusis, where the Earth-mother's temple stands. For there she met Triptolemus, when all the land lay waste, Demeter the kind Earth mother, and in her hands a sheaf of corn. And she taught him to plough the fallows, and to yoke the lazy kine; and she taught him to sow the seed-fields, and to reap the golden grain; and sent him forth to teach all nations, and give corn to labouring men. So at Eleusis all men honour her, whosoever tills the land; her and Triptolemus her beloved, who gave corn to labouring men.

And he went along the plain into Eleusis, and stood in the market-place, and cried—

"Where is Kerkuon, the king of the city? I must wrestle a fall with him to-day."

Then all the people crowded round him, and

cried, "Fair youth, why will you die? Hasten out of the city, before the cruel king hears that a stranger is here."

But Theseus went up through the town, while the people wept and prayed, and through the gates of the palace-yard, and through the piles of bones and skulls, till he came to the door ot Kerkuon's hall, the terror of all mortal men.

And there he saw Kerkuon sitting at the table in the hall alone; and before him was a whole sheep roasted, and beside him a whole jar of wine. And Theseus stood and called him, "Holla, thou valiant wrestler, wilt thou wrestle a fall to-day?"

And Kerkuon looked up and laughed, and answered, "I will wrestle a fall to-day; but come in, for I am lonely and thou weary, and eat and drink before thou die."

Then Theseus went up boldly, and sat down before Kerkuon at the board; and he ate his fill of the sheep's flesh, and drank his fill of the wine; and Theseus ate enough for three men, but Kerkuon ate enough for seven.

But neither spoke a word to the other, though they looked across the table by stealth;

and each said in his heart, "He has broad shoulders; but I trust mine are as broad as his."

At last, when the sheep was eaten and the jar of wine drained dry, King Kerkuon rose, and cried, "Let us wrestle a fall before we sleep."

So they tossed off all their garments, and went forth in the palace-yard; and Kerkuon bade strew fresh sand in an open space between the bones. And there the heroes stood face to face, while their eyes glared like wild bulls'; and all the people crowded at the gates to see what would befall.

And there they stood and wrestled, till the stars shone out above their heads, up and down and round, till the sand was stamped hard beneath their feet. And their eyes flashed like stars in the darkness, and their breath went up like smoke in the night air; but neither took nor gave a footstep, and the people watched silent at the gates.

But at last Kerkuon grew angry, and caught Theseus round the neck, and shook him as a mastiff shakes a rat; but he could not shake him off his feet.

But Theseus was quick and wary, and clasped Kerkuon round the waist, and slipped his loin quickly underneath him, while he caught him by the wrist; and then he hove a mighty heave, a heave which would have stirred an oak, and lifted Kerkuon, and pitched him right over his shoulder on the ground.

Then he leapt on him, and called, " Yield, or I kill thee!" but Kerkuon said no word; for his heart was burst within him with the fall, and the meat, and the wine.

Then Theseus opened the gates, and called in all the people; and they cried, " You have slain our evil king; be you now our king, and rule us well."

" I will be your king in Eleusis, and I will rule you right and well; for this cause I have slain all evil-doers—Sinis, and Sciron, and this man last of all."

Then an aged man stepped forth, and said, " Young hero, hast thou slain Sinis? Beware then of Ægeus, king of Athens, to whom thou goest, for he is near of kin to Sinis."

" Then I have slain my own kinsman," said Theseus, " though well he deserved to die. Who will purge me from his death, for rightfully I slew him, unrighteous and accursed as he was ? "

And the old man answered—

"That will the heroes do, the sons of Phytalus, who dwell beneath the elm-tree in Aphidnai, by the bank of silver Cephisus; for they know the mysteries of the Gods. Thither you shall go and be purified, and after you shall be our king"

So he took an oath of the people of Eleusis, that they would serve him as their king, and went away next morning across the Thriasian plain, and over the hills toward Aphidnai, that he might find the sons of Phytalus.

And as he was skirting the Vale of Cephisus, along the foot of lofty Parnes, a very tall and strong man came down to meet him, dressed in rich garments. On his arms were golden bracelets, and round his neck a collar of jewels; and he came forward, bowing courteously, and held out both his hands, and spoke—

"Welcome, fair youth, to these mountains; happy am I to have met you! For what greater pleasure to a good man than to entertain strangers? But I see that you are weary. Come up to my castle, and rest yourself awhile."

"I give you thanks," said Theseus : "but I am in haste to go up the valley, and to reach Aphidnai in the Vale of Cephisus."

"Alas! you have wandered far from the right way, and you cannot reach Aphidnai to-night, for there are many miles of mountain between you and it, and steep passes, and cliffs dangerous after nightfall. It is well for you that I met you, for my whole joy is to find strangers, and to feast them at my castle, and hear tales from them of foreign lands. Come up with me, and eat the best of venison, and drink the rich red wine, and sleep upon my famous bed, of which all travellers say that they never saw the like. For whatsoever the stature of my guest, however tall or short, that bed fits him to a hair, and he sleeps on it as he never slept before." And he laid hold on Theseus' hands, and would not let him go.

Theseus wished to go forwards : but he was ashamed to seem churlish to so hospitable a man; and he was curious to see that wondrous bed; and beside, he was hungry and weary : yet he shrank from the man, he knew not why; for, though his voice was gentle and fawning, it was dry and husky like a toad's; and though

his eyes were gentle, they were dull and cold
like stones. But he consented, and went with
the man up a glen which led from the road
toward the peaks of Parnes, under the dark
shadow of the cliffs.

And as they went up, the glen grew nar-
rower, and the cliffs higher and darker, and
beneath them a torrent roared, half seen between bare limestone crags. And around them
was neither tree nor bush, while from the white
peaks of Parnes the snow-blasts swept down
the glen, cutting and chilling, till a horror fell
on Theseus as he looked round at that doleful
place. And he asked at last, "Your castle
stands, it seems, in a dreary region?"

"Yes; but once within it, hospitality makes
all things cheerful. But who are these?" and
he looked back, and Theseus also; and far below, along the road which they had left, came
a string of laden asses, and merchants walking
by them, watching their ware.

"Ah, poor souls!" said the stranger. "Well
for them that I looked back and saw them!
And well for me too, for I shall have the more
guests at my feast. Wait awhile till I go down
and call them, and we will eat and drink to-

gether the livelong night. Happy am I, to whom Heaven sends so many guests at once!"

And he ran back down the hill, waving his hand and shouting to the merchants, while Theseus went slowly up the steep pass.

But as he went up he met an aged man, who had been gathering driftwood in the torrent-bed. He had laid down his faggot in the road, and was trying to lift it again to his shoulder. And when he saw Theseus, he called to him, and said—

"O fair youth, help me up with my burden, for my limbs are stiff and weak with years."

Then Theseus lifted the burden on his back. And the old man blest him, and then looked earnestly upon him, and said—

"Who are you, fair youth, and wherefore travel you this doleful road?"

"Who I am my parents know; but I travel this doleful road because I have been invited by a hospitable man, who promises to feast me, and to make me sleep upon I know not what wondrous bed."

Then the old man clapped his hands together and cried—

"O house of Hades, man-devouring! will

thy maw never be full? Know, fair youth, that
you are going to torment and to death, for he
who met you (I will requite your kindness by
another) is a robber and a murderer of men.
Whatsoever stranger he meets he entices him
hither to death; and as for this bed of which
he speaks, truly it fits all comers, yet none ever
rose alive off it save me."

"Why?" asked Theseus, astonished.

"Because, if a man be too tall for it, he lops
his limbs till they be short enough, and if he
be too short, he stretches his limbs till they be
long enough: but me only he spared, seven
weary years agone; for I alone of all fitted his
bed exactly, so he spared me, and made me his
slave. And once I was a wealthy merchant,
and dwelt in brazen-gated Thebes; but now I
hew wood and draw water for him, the torment
of all mortal men."

Then Theseus said nothing; but he ground
his teeth together.

"Escape, then," said the old man, "for he
will have no pity on thy youth. But yester-
day he brought up hither a young man and a
maiden, and fitted them upon his bed; and
the young man's hands and feet he cut off, but

the maiden's limbs he stretched until she died, and so both perished miserably—but I am tired of weeping over the slain. And therefore he is called Procrustes the stretcher, though his father called him Damastes. Flee from him : yet whither will you flee ? The cliffs are steep, and who can climb them ? and there is no other road."

But Theseus laid his hand upon the old man's mouth, and said, "There is no need to flee ;" and he turned to go down the pass.

"Do not tell him that I have warned you, or he will kill me by some evil death ;" and the old man screamed after him down the glen; but Theseus strode on in his wrath.

And he said to himself, "This is an ill-ruled land ; when shall I have done ridding it of monsters ?" And as he spoke, Procrustes came up the hill, and all the merchants with him, smiling and talking gaily. And when he saw Theseus, he cried, "Ah, fair young guest, have I kept you too long waiting ?"

But Theseus answered, "The man who stretches his guests upon a bed and hews off their hands and feet, what shall be done to him when right is done throughout the land ?"

P

Then Procrustes' countenance changed, and his cheeks grew as green as a lizard, and he felt for his sword in haste; but Theseus leapt on him, and cried—

"Is this true, my host, or is it false?" and he clasped Procrustes round waist and elbow, so that he could not draw his sword.

"Is this true, my host, or is it false?" But Procrustes answered never a word.

Then Theseus flung him from him, and lifted up his dreadful club; and before Procrustes could strike him he had struck, and felled him to the ground.

And once again he struck him; and his evil soul fled forth, and went down to Hades squeaking, like a bat into the darkness of a cave.

Then Theseus stript him of his gold ornaments, and went up to his house, and found there great wealth and treasure, which he had stolen from the passers-by. And he called the people of the country, whom Procrustes had spoiled a long time, and parted the spoil among them, and went down the mountains, and away.

And he went down the glens of Parnes,

through mist, and cloud, and rain, down the slopes of oak, and lentisk, and arbutus, and fragrant bay, till he came to the Vale of Cephisus, and the pleasant town of Aphidnai, and the home of the Phytalid heroes, where they dwelt beneath a mighty elm.

And there they built an altar, and bade him bathe in Cephisus, and offer a yearling ram, and purified him from the blood of Sinis, and sent him away in peace.

And he went down the valley by Acharnai, and by the silver-swirling stream, while all the people blessed him, for the fame of his prowess had spread wide, till he saw the plain of Athens, and the hill where Athené dwells.

So Theseus went up through Athens, and all the people ran out to see him; for his fame had gone before him, and every one knew of his mighty deeds. And all cried, "Here comes the hero who slew Sinis, and Phaia the wild sow of Crommyon, and conquered Kerkuon in wrestling, and slew Procrustes the pitiless." But Theseus went on sadly and steadfastly, for his heart yearned after his father; and he said, "How shall I deliver him from these leeches who suck his blood?"

So he went up the holy stairs, and into the Acropolis, where Ægeus' palace stood ; and he went straight into Ægeus' hall, and stood upon the threshold, and looked round.

And there he saw his cousins sitting about the table at the wine : many a son of Pallas, but no Ægeus among them. There they sat and feasted, and laughed, and passed the wine-cup round ; while harpers harped, and slave-girls sang, and the tumblers showed their tricks.

Loud laughed the sons of Pallas, and fast went the wine-cup round ; but Theseus frowned, and said under his breath, " No wonder that the land is full of robbers, while such as these bear rule."

Then the Pallantids saw him, and called to him, half-drunk with wine, " Holla, tall stranger at the door, what is your will to-day ? "

" I come hither to ask for hospitality."

" Then take it, and welcome. You look like a hero and a bold warrior ; and we like such to drink with us."

" I ask no hospitality of you ; I ask it of Ægeus the king, the master of this house."

At that some growled, and some laughed,

and shouted "Heyday! we are all masters here."

"Then I am master as much as the rest of you," said Theseus, and he strode past the table up the hall, and looked around for Ægeus; but he was nowhere to be seen.

The Pallantids looked at him, and then at each other; and each whispered to the man next him, "This is a forward fellow; he ought to be thrust out at the door." But each man's neighbour whispered in return, "His shoulders are broad; will you rise and put him out?" So they all sat still where they were.

Then Theseus called to the servants, and said, "Go tell King Ægeus, your master, that Theseus of Trœzene is here, and asks to be his guest awhile."

A servant ran and told Ægeus, where he sat in his chamber within, by Medeia the dark witch-woman, watching her eye and hand. And when Ægeus heard of Trœzene he turned pale and red again, and rose from his seat trembling, while Medeia watched him like a snake.

"What is Trœzene to you?" she asked. But he said hastily, "Do you not know who this Theseus is? The hero who has cleared the country from all monsters; but that he came from Trœzene, I never heard before. I must go out and welcome him."

So Ægeus came out into the hall; and when Theseus saw him, his heart leapt into his mouth, and he longed to fall on his neck and welcome him; but he controlled himself, and said, "My father may not wish for me, after all. I will try him before I discover myself;" and he bowed low before Ægeus, and said, "I have delivered the king's realm from many monsters; therefore I am come to ask a reward of the king."

And old Ægeus looked on him, and loved him, as what fond heart would not have done? But he only sighed, and said—

"It is little that I can give you, noble lad, and nothing that is worthy of you; for surely you are no mortal man, or at least no mortal's son."

"All I ask," said Theseus, "is to eat and drink at your table."

"That I can give you," said Ægeus, "if at least I am master in my own hall."

Then he bade them put a seat for Theseus,

and set before him the best of the feast; and
Theseus sat and ate so much, that all the
company wondered at him: but always he
kept his club by his side.

But Medeia the dark witch-woman had
been watching him all the while. She saw
how Ægeus turned red and pale when the lad
said that he came from Trœzene. She saw,
too, how his heart was opened toward Theseus;
and how Theseus bore himself before all the
sons of Pallas, like a lion among a pack of
curs. And she said to herself, "This youth
will be master here; perhaps he is nearer to
Ægeus already than mere fancy. At least the
Pallantids will have no chance by the side
of such as he."

Then she went back into her chamber
modestly, while Theseus ate and drank; and
all the servants whispered, "This, then, is the
man who killed the monsters! How noble are
his looks, and how huge his size! Ah, would
that he were our master's son!"

But presently Medeia came forth, decked
in all her jewels, and her rich Eastern robes,
and looking more beautiful than the day, so
that all the guests could look at nothing else.

And in her right hand she held a golden cup, and in her left a flask of gold; and she came up to Theseus, and spoke in a sweet, soft, winning voice—

"Hail to the hero, the conqueror, the unconquered, the destroyer of all evil things! Drink, hero, of my charmed cup, which gives rest after every toil, which heals all wounds, and pours new life into the veins. Drink of my cup, for in it sparkles the wine of the East, and Nepenthe, the comfort of the Immortals."

And, as she spoke, she poured the flask into the cup; and the fragrance of the wine spread through the hall, like the scent of thyme and roses.

And Theseus looked up in her fair face and into her deep dark eyes. And as he looked, he shrank and shuddered; for they were dry like the eyes of a snake. And he rose, and said, "The wine is rich and fragrant, and the wine-bearer as fair as the Immortals; but let her pledge me first herself in the cup, that the wine may be the sweeter from her lips."

Then Medeia turned pale, and stammered, "Forgive me, fair hero; but I am ill, and dare drink no wine."

And Theseus looked again into her eyes, and cried, "Thou shalt pledge me in that cup, or die." And he lifted up his brazen club, while all the guests looked on aghast.

Medeia shrieked a fearful shriek, and dashed the cup to the ground, and fled; and where the wine flowed over the marble pavement, the stone bubbled, and crumbled, and hissed, under the fierce venom of the draught.

But Medeia called her dragon chariot, and sprang into it and fled aloft, away over land and sea, and no man saw her more.

And Ægeus cried, "What hast thou done?" But Theseus pointed to the stone, "I have rid the land of an enchantment: now I will rid it of one more."

And he came close to Ægeus, and drew from his bosom the sword and the sandals, and said the words which his mother bade him.

And Ægeus stepped back a pace, and looked at the lad till his eyes grew dim; and then he cast himself on his neck and wept, and Theseus wept on his neck, till they had no strength left to weep more.

Then Ægeus turned to all the people, and cried, "Behold my son, children of Cecrops, a better man than his father was before him."

Who, then, were mad but the Pallantids, though they had been mad enough before? And one shouted, "Shall we make room for an upstart, a pretender, who comes from we know not where?" And another, "If he be one, we are more than one; and the stronger can hold his own." And one shouted one thing, and one another; for they were hot and wild with wine; but all caught swords and lances off the wall, where the weapons hung around, and sprang forward to Theseus, and Theseus sprang forward to them.

And he cried, "Go in peace, if you will, my cousins; but if not, your blood be on your own heads." But they rushed at him; and then stopped short and railed him, as curs stop and bark when they rouse a lion from his lair.

But one hurled a lance from the rear rank, which past close by Theseus' head; and at that Theseus rushed forward, and the fight began indeed. Twenty against one they fought, and yet Theseus beat them all; and those who were left fled down into the town, where the people set on them, and drove them out, till Theseus was left alone in the palace, with Ægeus his new-found father. But before nightfall all the town came up, with victims, and dances, and songs; and they offered sacrifices to Athené, and rejoiced all the night long, because their king had found a noble son, and an heir to his royal house.

So Theseus stayed with his father all the winter; and when the spring equinox drew near, all the Athenians grew sad and silent, and Theseus saw it, and asked the reason, but no one would answer him a word.

Then he went to his father, and asked him: but Ægeus turned away his face and wept.

"Do not ask, my son, beforehand, about evils which must happen: it is enough to have to face them when they come."

And when the spring equinox came, a herald came to Athens, and stood in the market, and cried, "O people and King of Athens, where is your yearly tribute?" Then a great lamentation arose throughout the city. But Theseus stood up to the herald, and cried—

"And who are you, dog-faced, who dare

demand tribute here? If I did not reverence your herald's staff, I would brain you with this club."

And the herald answered proudly, for he was a grave and ancient man—

"Fair youth, I am not dog-faced or shameless; but I do my master's bidding. Minos, the King of hundred-citied Crete, the wisest of all kings on earth. And you must be surely a stranger here, or you would know why I come, and that I come by right."

"I am a stranger here. Tell me, then, why you come."

"To fetch the tribute which King Ægeus promised to Minos, and confirmed his promise with an oath. For Minos conquered all this land, and Megara which lies to the east, when he came hither with a great fleet of ships, enraged about the murder of his son. For his son Androgeos came hither to the Panathenaic games, and overcame all the Greeks in the sports, so that the people honoured him as a hero. But when Ægeus saw his valour, he envied him, and feared lest he should join the sons of Pallas, and take away the sceptre from him. So he plotted against his life, and slew him basely, no man knows how or where. Some say that he waylaid him by Oinoe, on the road which goes to Thebes; and some that he sent him against the bull of Marathon, that the beast might kill him. But Ægeus says that the young men killed him from envy, because he had conquered them in the games. So Minos came hither and avenged him, and would not depart till this land had promised him tribute—seven youths and seven maidens every year, who go with me in a black-sailed ship, till they come to hundred-citied Crete."

And Theseus ground his teeth together, and said, "Wert thou not a herald I would kill thee for saying such things of my father; but I will go to him, and know the truth." So he went to his father, and asked him; but he turned away his head and wept, and said, "Blood was shed in the land unjustly, and by blood it is avenged. Break not my heart by questions; it is enough to endure in silence."

Then Theseus groaned inwardly, and said, "I will go myself with these youths and maidens, and kill Minos upon his royal throne."

And Ægeus shrieked, and cried, "You shall not go, my son, the light of my old age,

to whom alone I look to rule this people after
I am dead and gone.   You shall not go, to die
horribly, as those youths and maidens die; for
Minos thrusts them into a labyrinth, which
Daidalos made for him among the rocks,—
Daidalos the renegade, the accursed, the pest
of this his native land.   From that labyrinth
no one can escape, entangled in its winding
ways, before they meet the Minotaur, the
monster who feeds upon the flesh of men.
There he devours them horribly, and they
never see this land again."

Then Theseus grew red, and his ears
tingled, and his heart beat loud in his bosom.
And he stood awhile like a tall stone pillar on
the cliffs above some hero's grave; and at last
he spoke—

"Therefore all the more I will go with them,
and slay the accursed beast.   Have I not slain
all evil-doers and monsters, that I might free
this land?   Where are Periphetes, and Sinis,
and Kerkuon, and Phaia the wild sow?
Where are the fifty sons of Pallas?   And this
Minotaur shall go the road which they have
gone, and Minos himself, if he dare stay me."

"But how will you slay him, my son?   For

you must leave your club and your armour
behind, and be cast to the monster, defenceless
and naked like the rest."

And Theseus said, "Are there no stones in
that labyrinth; and have I not fists and teeth?
Did I need my club to kill Kerkuon, the terror
of all mortal men?"

Then Ægeus clung to his knees; but he
would not hear; and at last he let him go,
weeping bitterly, and said only this one word—

"Promise me but this, if you return in peace,
though that may hardly be: take down the
black sail of the ship (for I shall watch for it all
day upon the cliffs), and hoist instead a white
sail, that I may know afar off that you are safe."

And Theseus promised, and went out, and to
the market-place where the herald stood, while
they drew lots for the youths and maidens, who
were to sail in that doleful crew. And the
people stood wailing and weeping, as the lot
fell on this one and on that; but Theseus strode
into the midst, and cried—

"Here is a youth who needs no lot. I
myself will be one of the seven."

And the herald asked in wonder, "Fair
youth, know you whither you are going?"

And Theseus said, " I know. Let us go down to the black-sailed ship."

So they went down to the black-sailed ship, seven maidens, and seven youths, and Theseus before them all, and the people following them lamenting. But Theseus whispered to his companions, " Have hope, for the monster is not immortal. Where are Periphetes, and Sinis, and Sciron, and all whom I have slain ?" Then their hearts were comforted a little ; but they wept as they went on board, and the cliffs of Sunium rang, and all the isles of the Ægean Sea, with the voice of their lamentation, as they sailed on toward their deaths in Crete.

PART III

HOW THESEUS SLEW THE MINOTAUR

AND at last they came to Crete, and to Cnossus, beneath the peaks of Ida, and to the palace of Minos the great king, to whom Zeus himself taught laws. So he was the wisest of all mortal kings, and conquered all the Ægean isles; and his ships were as many as the sea-gulls, and his palace like a marble hill. And he sat among the pillars of the hall, upon his throne of beaten gold, and around him stood the speaking statues which Daidalos had made by his skill. For Daidalos was the most cunning of all Athenians, and he first invented the plumb-line, and the auger, and glue, and many a tool with which wood is wrought. And he first set up masts in ships, and yards, and his son made sails for them: but Perdix his nephew excelled him; for he first invented the saw and its teeth, copying it from the back-bone of a fish ; and invented, too, the chisel, and the compasses, and the potter's wheel which moulds the clay. Therefore Daidalos envied him, and hurled him headlong from the temple of Athené ; but the Goddess pitied him (for she loves the wise), and changed him into a partridge, which flits for ever about the hills. And Daidalos fled to Crete, to Minos, and worked for him many a year, till he did a shameful deed, at which the sun hid his face on high.

Then he fled from the anger of Minos, he and Icaros his son having made themselves wings of feathers, and fixed the feathers with wax. So they flew over the sea toward Sicily ; but Icaros flew too near the sun ; and the wax of his wings was melted, and he fell into the Icarian Sea. But Daidalos came safe to Sicily, and there wrought many a wondrous work ; for he made for King Cocalos a reservoir, from which a great river watered all the land, and a castle and a treasury on a mountain, which the giants themselves could not have stormed ; and in Selinos he took the steam which comes up from the fires of Ætna, and made of it a warm bath of vapour, to cure the pains of mortal men ; and he made a honeycomb of gold, in which the bees came and stored their honey, and in Egypt he made the forecourt of the temple of Hephaistos in Memphis, and a statue of himself within it, and many another wondrous work. And for Minos he made statues which spoke and moved, and the temple of Britomartis, and the dancing-hall of Ariadne, which he carved of fair white stone And in Sardinia he worked for Iölaos, and in many a land beside, wandering up and down for ever with his cunning, unlovely and accursed by men.

But Theseus stood before Minos, and they looked each other in the face. And Minos bade take them to prison, and cast them to the monster one by one, that the death of Androgeos might be avenged. Then Theseus cried—

"A boon, O Minos ! Let me be thrown first to the beast. For I came hither for that very purpose, of my own will, and not by lot."

"Who art thou, then, brave youth ? "

" I am the son of him whom of all men thou hatest most, Ægeus the king of Athens, and I am come here to end this matter."

And Minos pondered awhile, looking steadfastly at him, and he thought, "The lad means to atone by his own death for his father's sin;" and he answered at last mildly—

"Go back in peace, my son. It is a pity that one so brave should die."

But Theseus said, "I have sworn that I will not go back till I have seen the monster face to face."

And at that Minos frowned, and said, "Then thou shalt see him; take the madman away."

And they led Theseus away into the prison, with the other youths and maids.

But Ariadne, Minos' daughter, saw him, as she came out of her white stone hall; and she loved him for his courage and his majesty, and said, "Shame that such a youth should die!" And by night she went down to the prison, and told him all her heart; and said—

"Flee down to your ship at once, for I have bribed the guards before the door. Flee, you and all your friends, and go back in peace to Greece; and take me, take me with you! for I dare not stay after you are gone; for my father will kill me miserably, if he knows what I have done."

And Theseus stood silent awhile; for he was astonished and confounded by her beauty: but at last he said, " I cannot go home in peace, till I have seen and slain this Minotaur, and avenged the deaths of the youths and maidens, and put an end to the terrors of my land."

" And will you kill the Minotaur ? How, then ? "

" I know not, nor do I care : but he must be strong if he be too strong for me."

Then she loved him all the more, and said, " But when you have killed him, how will you find your way out of the labyrinth ? "

" I know not, neither do I care : but it must be a strange road, if I do not find it out before I have eaten up the monster's carcase."

Then she loved him all the more, and said—

" Fair youth, you are too bold; but I can help you, weak as I am. I will give you a sword, and with that perhaps you may slay the beast; and a clue of thread, and by that, perhaps, you may find your way out again. Only promise me that if you escape safe you will take me home with you to Greece; for my father will surely kill me, if he knows what I have done."

"Then Theseus laughed, and said, "Am I not safe enough now?" And he hid the sword in his bosom, and rolled up the clue in his hand; and then he swore to Ariadne, and fell down before her, and kissed her hands and her feet; and she wept over him a long while, and then went away; and Theseus lay down and slept sweetly.

And when the evening came, the guards came in and led him away to the labyrinth.

And he went down into that doleful gulf, through winding paths among the rocks, under caverns, and arches, and galleries, and over heaps of fallen stone. And he turned on the left hand, and on the right hand, and went up and down, till his head was dizzy; but all the while he held his clue. For when he went in he had fastened it to a stone, and left it to unroll out of his hand as he went on; and it lasted him till he met the Minotaur, in a narrow chasm between black cliffs.

And when he saw him he stopped awhile, for he had never seen so strange a beast. His body was a man's: but his head was the head of a bull; and his teeth were the teeth of a lion; and with them he tore his prey. And when he saw Theseus he roared, and put his head down, and rushed right at him.

But Theseus stept aside nimbly, and as he passed by, cut him in the knee; and ere he could turn in the narrow path, he followed him, and stabbed him again and again from behind, till the monster fled bellowing wildly; for he never before had felt a wound. And Theseus followed him at full speed, holding the clue of thread in his left hand.

Then on, through cavern after cavern, under dark ribs of sounding stone, and up rough glens and torrent-beds, among the sunless roots of Ida, and to the edge of the eternal snow, went they, the hunter and the hunted, while the hills bellowed to the monster's bellow.

And at last Theseus came up with him, where he lay panting on a slab among the snow, and caught him by the horns, and forced his head back, and drove the keen sword through his throat.

Then he turned, and went back limping and weary, feeling his way down by the clue of thread, till he came to the mouth of that doleful place; and saw waiting for him, whom but Ariadne!

And he whispered "It is done!" and showed her the sword, and she laid her finger on her lips, and led him to the prison, and opened the doors, and set all the prisoners free, while the guards lay sleeping heavily; for she had silenced them with wine.

Then they fled to their ship together, and leapt on board, and hoisted up the sail; and the night lay dark around them, so that they passed through Minos' ships, and escaped all safe to Naxos; and there Ariadne became Theseus' wife.

ARIADNE

(From the Statue in the Vatican.

The Young

PART IV

HOW THESEUS FELL BY HIS PRIDE

BUT that fair Ariadne never came to Athens with her husband. Some say that Theseus left her sleeping on Naxos among the Cyclades; and that Dionusos the wine-king found her, and took her up into the sky, as you shall see some day in a painting of old Titian's—one of the most glorious pictures upon earth. And some say that Dionusos drove away Theseus, and took Ariadne from him by force: but however that may be, in his haste or in his grief, Theseus forgot to put up the white sail. Now Ægeus his father sat and watched on Sunium day after day, and strained his old eyes across the sea to see the ship afar. And when he saw the black sail, and not the white one, he gave up Theseus for dead, and in his grief he fell into the sea, and died; so it is called the Ægean to this day.

And now Theseus was king of Athens, and he guarded it and ruled it well.

For he killed the bull of Marathon, which had killed Androgeos, Minos' son; and he drove back the famous Amazons, the warlike women of the East, when they came from Asia, and conquered all Hellas, and broke into Athens itself. But Theseus stopped them there, and conquered them, and took Hippolyte their queen to be his wife. Then he went out to fight against the Lapithai, and Peirithoos their famous king: but when the two heroes came face to face they loved each other, and embraced, and became noble friends; so that the friendship of Theseus and Peirithoos is a proverb even now. And he gathered (so the Athenians say) all the boroughs of the land together, and knit them into one strong people, while before they were all parted and weak: and many another wise thing he did, so that his people honoured him after he was dead, for many a hundred years, as the father of their freedom and their laws. And six hundred years after his death, in the famous fight at Marathon, men said that they saw the ghost of Theseus, with his mighty brazen club, fighting in the van of battle against the invading Persians, for the country which he loved. And twenty years after Marathon his bones (they say) were found in Scuros, an isle beyond the sea; and they were bigger than the bones of mortal man. So the Athenians brought them home in triumph; and all the people came out to welcome them; and they built over them a noble temple, and adorned it with sculptures and paintings; in which we are told all the noble deeds of Theseus, and the Centaurs, and the Lapithai, and the Amazons; and the ruins of it are standing still.

But why did they find his bones in Scuros? Why did he not die in peace at Athens, and sleep by his father's side? Because after his triumph he grew proud, and broke the laws of God and man. And one thing worst of all he did, which brought him to his grave with sorrow. For he went down (they say beneath the earth) with that bold Peirithoos his friend to help him to carry off Persephone, the queen of the world below. But Peirithoos

was killed miserably, in the dark fire king-
doms under ground; and Theseus was chained
to a rock in everlasting pain. And there he
sat for years, till Heracles the mighty came
down to bring up the three-headed dog who
sits at Pluto's gate. So Heracles loosed him
from his chain, and brought him up to the
light once more.

But when he came back his people had
forgotten him, and Castor and Polydeuces, the
sons of the wondrous Swan, had invaded his
land, and carried off his mother Aithra for a
slave, in revenge for a grievous wrong.

So the fair land of Athens was wasted, and
another king ruled it, who drove out Theseus
shamefully, and he fled across the sea to
Scuros. And there he lived in sadness, in
the house of Lucomedes the king, till Lucomedes killed him by treachery, and there was
an end of all his labours.

So it is still, my children, and so it will be
to the end. In those old Greeks, and in us
also, all strength and virtue come from God.
But if men grow proud and self-willed, and
misuse God's fair gifts, He lets them go
their own ways, and fall pitifully, that the

glory may be His alone. God help us all, and give us wisdom, and courage to do noble deeds ! but God keep pride from us when we have done them, lest we fall, and come to shame !

THE END

Butler & Tanner, The Selwood Printing Works, Frome, and London.

NEW 2/= SERIES...
...OF GIFT BOOKS.

Large Crown 8vo, cloth gilt, Illustrated.

THE names of the Authors give sufficient guarantee of the literary merits and interest of these Books, whilst for selling value the line will be found unequalled in Copyright Books. Paper, printing, binding, and illustrations are alike excellent.

———

1 **The Mids of the "Rattlesnake."**
   By ARTHUR LEE KNIGHT. Illustrated by W. S. STACEY.

2 **The Black Man's Ghost.**
   By JOHN C. HUTCHESON. Illustrated by W. S. STACEY.

3 **Dicky Beaumont.**
   By ARTHUR LEE KNIGHT. Illustrated by W. S. STACEY.

4 **The Heir of Langridge Towers.**
   By R. M. FREEMAN. Illustrated by W. S. STACEY.

5 **Frank Allreddy's Fortune.**
   By CAPTAIN FRANKLIN FOX. Illustrated by W. S. STACEY.

6 **The Rajah of Monkey Island.**
   By ARTHUR LEE KNIGHT. Illustrated by W. S. STACEY.

7 **The Cruise of the "Cormorant."**
   By ARTHUR LEE KNIGHT. Illustrated by W. S. STACEY.

8 **Westward Ho!**
   By CHARLES KINGSLEY. Illustrated by HENRY AUSTIN.

———

WARD, LOCK & CO., LIMITED.

9 **Silas, the Conjurer.**
   By JAMES GREENWOOD. Fully Illustrated in the text.

10 **From Log Cabin to White House.**
   By W. M. THAYER.

11 **Robinson Crusoe.** By DANIEL DEFOE.

12 **Bunyan's Pilgrim's Progress.**

13 **Grimm's Fairy Tales.**

14 **Arabian Nights Entertainments.**

15 **Swiss Family Robinson.**

16 **Andersen's Popular Tales.**

17 **Andersen's Stories.**

18 **Boys' Own Sea Stories.**

19 **Two Years Before the Mast.** R. H. DANA.

20 **The Scottish Chiefs.** By JANE PORTER.

21 **Ivanhoe.** By SIR WALTER SCOTT.

22 **Romance of Navigation.** By HENRY FRITH.

23 **Two Years Ago.** By CHARLES KINGSLEY.

24 **The Last of the Barons.** By BULWER LYTTON.

25 **Harold.** By BULWER LYTTON.

———

WARD, LOCK & CO., LIMITED.